HYBRIDS

Are you a slave to your computer?
Welded to your mobile phone?
Joined at the hip to your iPod?

Maybe, one day, you will be…

David Thorpe lives in the mountains not far from the beaches of beautiful mid-Wales. He spends his time wondering. When he was smaller he noticed that most adults seemed to have forgotten what it was like to be a child and vowed to try not to do the same himself. Previously he has worked on the sewers, written comics, published eco-books and been a journalist. If you want to make him happy you can help to save the tiger from extinction.

Hybrids was the winning entry in HarperCollins nationwide search for an author competition with Saga Magazine, beating a phenomenal 882 other manuscripts to first place.

......JOHNNY ONLINE'S BLOG...
...HYBRID NATION......

Declaration of the Rights of Hybrids

Hybrids are human:

Hybrids may be genetically changed, but we're still your children. The hybrids' cause is a cause for every human being, because anyone might catch the virus.

Society - you cannot abandon us.

Hybrids have equal rights:

When humans become hybrids they have to keep the same rights as healthy people. These rights are freedom, owning things, being safe and not being persecuted.

As with healthy humans, hybrids' freedom can only be limited by anything that might harm someone else or stop others being free in the same way. But if the government makes laws which give some members of society more rights than others, then those deprived of their rights must still be able to fight for those rights to be given back to them.

Hybrids must unite:

Hybrids have the natural right to expect that society will protect and help them. If the government doesn't respect this right, then hybrids must band together, for in togetherness is strength.

If the government does not protect us, then hybrids have no choice but to defend themselves, by any means at their disposal.

1. The Twisted Strands

As soon as I saw a beautiful girl pushing open the door, I remembered I'd arranged to meet her here. She hovered in the doorway, peering shyly around the gloom from beneath long dark eyebrows. Compared to everyone else in the dump she stood out like a sixth finger: flawless skin, tangled black curls, expensive Japanese clothes – a sense of style. Watching her, I felt in my genes that something was going to change. A rush in my circuits that said 'opportunity knocks'.

But I was scared of change. Change was not my friend.

I usually came to this backstreet café for losers called the Twisted Strands, because Francis, the owner, would let me buy just one drink and sit here for hours, no worries. Before I could compose myself the girl had sat down opposite and was trying to peer under my hood.

"Johnny Online?"

I grunted through my speakers.

"Am I late?"

"I wasn't keeping track of the time." I watched her getting used to the sound of my electronic voice and what serves for my face these days. "It's OK to stare," I said. "I'm used to it."

"I'm sorry," she blushed. "I'm a bit nervous. I've never met anyone I've chatted to online before. But this is an emergency."

"So you said," I replied, putting a flashing exclamation mark on my screen that reflected off her own face. I observed her confusion in its light; it was one of a number of reactions people have to the way I look. "Why not buy me another coffee and tell me all about it?"

She went to place an order. Francis handed her an all-day breakfast — juice, sausage, egg, toast — which she came back with and placed in front of me.

Too bad I couldn't eat it. I took out my flask, poured the juice in, connected my tube and began to suck it down. She didn't gawp like some.

"Don't worry," she said, "I'm used to strange habits."

"Oh yeah?" I asked.

"See?" She gave me a quick flash of her left arm,

slipping back the sleeve of her alpaca coat to reveal a mobile phone emerging from her hand. I saw her transition point: the way the flesh changed colour, texture and substance where her hand stopped being a hand.

"OK," I nodded. "I've seen a few of that type." I was suddenly sad for her. "Problem when you want to upgrade to a newer model, isn't it?"

She bit her lip.

"Sorry. Tact isn't my best feature." I tried to put a reassuring smile on my screen.

She began to tuck into the breakfast she'd bought me. "Look, I'm trusting you, just by being here. And you can trust me, so relax, Johnny. It's not as if I'm a Gene Police agent or anything. You know my name – Kestrella. It's French after my mother. Hey, your own point looks bad."

She'd been staring at where my skin turned into liquid crystals, just in front of my ears. I pulled my hood forwards.

"I don't have a mother," I blurted.

"But everyone has a mother!" she cried.

"Mine did a runner. When she saw what I'd become."

"Now it's my turn to say I'm sorry." She put her pale little hand on my mittened, grubby one. No one had done that for years.

I jerked it away. "I don't want to let you down, but… I-I have to go now."

I hurried out on to the tired street. Beneath the orange lights I pulled my hoodie tight around me. Keeping my head down I dodged the few pedestrians who were out, aware of her following me. I turned a corner on to the Walworth Road, my shoulders hunched. I was striding as fast as I could, but she was faster.

"'Hybrids must unite,'" she panted as she drew alongside me. "'We have the natural right to expect that society will protect and help us. If the government does not respect this right then we must band together, for in togetherness is strength…'"

The words seemed strangely familiar. Then I realised she was quoting something I'd written back at me. "'If the government does not protect us, then we have no choice but to defend ourselves…'" I continued.

"'…by any means at our disposal,'" she concluded, smiling. "It's from your blog, Hybrid Nation, isn't it? Declaration of the Rights of Hybrids? See – I've done my homework."

I stopped and put her face on close-up to see how earnest she was. So small. What kind of threat could she be either to me or to them? I was nearly two metres tall, but diminished by my stoop and by my charity-shop rags. Kestrella, on the other hand, was tiny but like a fashion model. "How come you can afford these clothes?" I asked.

"Find out," she challenged.

"Give us a clue," I protested. "I need something to go on."

She told me a name. I began an Internet search.

In a doorway, out of sight of passers-by, she read a new text on her mobile. Now I could clearly see where her transition occurred: the inflammation, raw like a weeping burn, and the strips of dead skin peeling off. It wasn't pleasant, but mine are worse.

I offered her my nearly used up can of De-Morph, but she declined.

"I have a better one," she said. "From Papa."

I examined the search results. She was Kestrella Chu, daughter of Sim Chu, marketing director for the big drug company Mu-Tech. It was the same name as on the tube from which she was now squeezing ointment on to her oozing skin. "Field-testing a new product, huh? So does Daddy know about… uh…?"

"Naturally." She fixed me with her eyes, big and brown, as if it was a challenge to my idea of reality. "But he chose not to give me up."

"You're a Blue?" I asked.

"Yes, he registered me. With my permission."

I looked around, puzzled. "Is he here then?"

She giggled. "Don't be silly. He's not my minder. He's far too busy!" She nodded across and down the street. On a side street leading off the main road I could just see a large 4x4 with shaded windows.

"You have a private minder?"

She nodded, smiling. "Hired specially for the job. His name is Dominic, and he is two metres tall and works out and weighs 85 kilos."

I put a white flag on my monitor. "O-kay," I said. "No worries. So, er, why does your father keep you at home then? Is it so he's got a real live guinea pig handy to test out his new products on?"

Her smile vanished and she left the doorway. "You really are a horrible cynic, aren't you?" It was my turn to try and keep up with her as she sped back up the road towards the 4x4. "Did life make you this way or is that the real reason your parents walked out on you?" I laughed for the first time in ages.

Running to catch up, the wind blew the hoodie off my head, revealing the monitor where my face should be. Two passers-by saw it – recoiled in fright, turned tail and ran the other way. I hurriedly pulled the hood well over my head and hoped they weren't off to call the Gene Police.

"Look," I was panting as I drew alongside Kestrella. "I'm fifteen years old, I should be in school, or losing my virginity, binge-drinking, skateboarding, or whatever it is boys my age do. But instead I've been living on the streets for two years, always on the lookout, trying to avoid things like that happening." I jerked my head back, one hand tugging my hood down tight over my monitor. "It's not surprising if I'm lacking a few airs and graces."

"You agreed to this rendezvous." She fixed me with a gaze. "And I need your help." She handed me her tube. Its brand name read I-So-L8. I squeezed out a dollop of cream and gingerly applied some to the side of my head where it hurt most. It felt good.

I looked at Kestrella, and how soft she was. Then I followed her across the road to the 4x4 with the smoky windows and we climbed into the back. As Dominic pulled away from the kerb and into the night, Kestrella opened a little fridge and began to feed stuff into my tube I hadn't tasted in years. Swirls of delicious fruit smoothies snaked into my stomach. I gazed at this girl who had everything, including acceptance, wondering if she could really be trusted, and what on earth she could want from me.

There was a block of ice in my heart and I had to stop it melting.

2. Exit From Nowheresville

I watched Johnny with an amused smile as he reacted to being inside Papa's vehicle: the smell of upholstered leather made supple with nap oil, the luxury of the satin cushions, the fridge containing energy drinks laced with spirulina and ginseng root. In short, a womb of mercy.

I leant forward. "Dominic," I told the driver. "We're going to see Cheri."

He steered north across the river. I told Johnny not to worry. No one could see us through the tinted windows.

To say he looked odd would be an understatement. It was shocking at first to see someone with no face; instead just a constantly shifting array of pixels obscuring his natural features. No eyes, no mouth, no nose. My mind conjured visions of how the rest of him might be transfigured.

But I was getting used to it surprisingly quickly. His lanky ginger hair concealed the piteous details of the transition. I felt a surge of pity for him. I'd got off lightly by comparison.

I liked how he used the screen to express his feelings in an ironic, witty way. When he'd removed his tube from the third bottle, a bloated smiley face appeared. I blew out my own cheeks and smiled back. I asked him if Johnny Online was his real name.

"No, it's something they gave me in a role-play game when I was eleven and it stuck after I got Creep. I don't want to remember my real name. I'm not the same person any more, know what I mean?" His voice was like a train announcement and seemed to come from beneath his chin. He'd chosen one that was neutral, mid-tone, with only slight inflection, perhaps deliberately to make himself like a robot. He continued: "When Creep hit I was eleven but I didn't catch it till I was twelve. I left home a year later."

I nodded. "Me too. But what a terrible story. You're a Grey, aren't you?"

"Yeah," he said proudly. "Don't know how but I've managed to stay unregistered for two years. I've learnt how to keep my head down."

He reached in the fridge again and started on a

strawberry yogurt. I couldn't believe how hungry he was. I tried to see where the tube went – it seemed to disappear into his throat through a hole in his neck.

"It must be terrible being a Grey," I prompted.

"It's probably better than being a Red though. The Gene Police take them to the Centre for Genetic Rehabilitation and they're never seen again."

The streets passed by outside: Russell Square, Camden High Street, all quiet. Dominic pulled over to let an armoured ambulance, its blue lights flashing, pass by. Johnny ducked instinctively.

"I know I've lived a rather sheltered life," I began hesitantly. For some reason I felt the need to apologise. "I can't begin to imagine what it's like to be homeless…"

I told him how I'd been protected by my parents' money and status, and until recently lived a life of careless ignorance. Then I too got the plague and began to find out how awful the world could be.

He listened to my story without comment. Then "Why pick me?" flashed on his screen with a picture of a blue face in a sea of yellow faces.

"I found your blog on the net. I–I thought you might be able to help me."

"Help you what? Find a cure?!" he snorted and flashed up a cartoon of a detective with a giant magnifying glass, then smashed it with a hammer. I smiled.

"No, that's Papa's company's job. But I'll tell you why later. First, we're going in here. Dominic?"

I'd timed it nicely. We were in West Hampstead and the car pulled up opposite a rambling, red-brick Victorian house with brown, smoked-glass extensions, surrounded by a few trees and a high security wall.

"Where are we?" asked Johnny.

"Don't you know?" I was surprised. "It's where they can help you."

"Hey. What makes you think I—"

"Oh, I'm sure you can remain anonymous if you like. A troubled soul checking in briefly from out of the cold. This is Salvation House."

"No way," he said petulantly.

"Oh, come on, Johnny. This is a hospice. It's run by my aunt. Everybody's heard of it. It's the most hybrid-friendly place in the country. The council's always threatening to close it down but they can't because there'd be a riot."

"Not interested," he intoned in an annoying, flat voice. His screen had gone blank.

"They'll clean you up, give you a medical…" I sighed. I didn't think he'd be like this. "Look at the state of you. You could die on the streets any day. The vigilante gangs, no money—"

"I can look after myself."

He kept saying this until I got the message. But Sally House was so nice. It was cosy and right at the heart of the struggle for the rights of Creep victims. My Aunt Cheri treated it as her family, her cause. Her heart was as big as London. He'd no right to turn down my offer of help. It could only be because he didn't know how marvellous it was. He registered my disappointment. His screen came alive again with a picture of wild mountains and clouds. A wolf howled at the sky. Was this how he really saw himself?

"Very well," I said coldly. "Can we drop you off somewhere?"

"Home."

"Home?" I didn't think he had a home.

He gave the location to Dominic, who impassively restarted the engine and took the car away from West Hampstead, back, back towards the river.

Johnny didn't want to know what I wanted to ask him to do. I felt hurt by his lack of curiosity. I'd been wrong about him. He was perverse. Perhaps he was more machine than boy. There was no heart beating beneath his synthetic casing. He'd been claimed by the creeping inorganic world. No amount of care could warm a heart that didn't exist.

There was a sullen silence throughout the journey.

I walked with him from the car along the side street. We were in a nowheresville, the anywhere of a 1930s suburban estate.

It had seen better times; the hedges straggled, untrimmed. Grime sucked the colour from all surfaces. Lace curtains drifted, ragged and unwashed. Litter snagged in the weed-claimed flower beds. Grey pebbledashing, like an old mask, had fallen from walls to reveal the shame of naked brickwork.

"You live here?" I asked.

"Sure. I like it. It suits me. See? Leaky houses once full of happy young families. The only things living here now are ghosts." And he explained how what he called their old comfort blanket had changed into a blanket of fear. "Who knows when this happened? Sometimes I think it began when they tarmacked the front gardens for their second or third cars, or perhaps it was when the kids and their mums and dads stopped playing together and disappeared into their bedrooms for hours on end to play computer games, watch TV, press buttons. Anyway, conversation stopped. Then I imagine how the children left, sucked down telephone wires or satellite cables into another dimension. Hear it now? No sound, no wind, no movement, no people. Just planes passing overhead and the distant complaints of sirens. Here we are," he announced.

It was a dark, semi-detached house with its windows and doors all boarded up. I held my nose against the stench of blocked drains. We clambered through a hole in a board nailed over the back door. Johnny threw a connection switch on an electricity meter, telling me he'd wired it to a street lamp outside – free electricity. "Don't know why everyone doesn't do this."

The lights blazed on and the blackness shrank into sharp shadows. I couldn't hide my shock. He took my hand as I stumbled over rubbish on the floor – wet, broken plaster, rotten floorboards, plastic bags, empty bottles.

"But what is this?" I asked naively.

"A squat, of course," he said, and I could tell that if his voice had been human, it would have betrayed a trace of contempt at my ignorance. "How d'you think I survived for two years?"

"I have no idea," I said.

"The first few weeks were the worst. Looking back, I was lucky I wasn't killed. One night I slept in the middle of a traffic island! I hid in the bushes, but it was hard to sleep cos of the noise."

"That's awful!"

"Then I met this guy, Turney. He was older, been homeless a while. He kind of took me under his wing. Saved my life really. Took me down to Southwark and found me a squat – the first of a string of them. To begin with I was sharing with about twenty others. At least I'm alone here. Turney showed me where you could get free food and clothes, and who was dangerous and who would be friendly. You see, there are cafés and shops which don't mind hybrids coming in; some are even run by hybrids. He showed me how to keep away from the vigilantes who come hunting for us, the Gene Police, the drug pushers and the pimps."

"Was he a hybrid?" I asked.

"No. But he kind of liked hanging out with them. He was about twenty, but he seemed a lot older. He used to say, 'Johnny-boy, if I'm going to get it, I'm going to get it. Don't matter what I do, my number will be up. So I ain't going to let some crummy virus scare me'."

Johnny led me upstairs: there were no carpets and our footsteps seemed too loud.

"He sounds nice. What happened to him?"

"Dunno. One day he just disappeared and I never saw him again. I looked for him at his usual haunts, but I never found him. Maybe he was picked up by the Gene

Police and sent to the CGR just for the hell of it."

Suddenly he froze. He signalled me to be silent. I could see daylight coming in from a bedroom. We continued slowly, treading on smashed glass. Johnny rushed into the back bedroom and I followed.

The room had been ransacked. I pinched my nose at the smell and saw excrement was smeared on the furniture. Graffiti on the walls shouted "Bye bye freaks"; "We'll get you next time"; "Hybrid control – mission accomplished". I saw Johnny stagger and rushed to support him, easing him on to a chair.

"My computers… back-ups… all gone…" he said. Equipment lay smashed on the floor. Papers were everywhere.

"What a mess," I said. "Do you know who did it?"

He looked at me as if he'd forgotten I was there.

"What does it matter?"

"Did they take much?"

"All my files – writing. My databases, programs, all my hardware… No, not much."

"Haven't you got it backed up somewhere?"

"Well, yes and no. Some of it, almost, a bit." On his screen a picture of an underground cave system momentarily replaced his standard screensaver of a stoned smiley face.

I began to poke around in the mess. "Good riddance to bad rubbish, no?"

"Yeah, but it was my rubbish."

"At least you weren't here when it happened."

"I can look after myself."

"I don't think so. Come on." I took a last look round, picked up a few papers and marched out of the bedroom. This time, he followed.

It was when we got into the front yard that they pounced. I think there were three of them. They must have only just left the house when we arrived, and had seen us, returning for an ambush. Screaming, they charged at us from the side passage, waving baseball bats and a crowbar.

I let out a shriek, grabbing Johnny's hand instinctively. We ran towards the gate, hotly pursued just a few metres behind.

But Dominic had seen what was happening and had coasted the car up to the house. The 4x4's brilliant lights flashed on and with a scream of tyres he swerved it across the road on to the pavement to illuminate fully the front garden.

Startled, our attackers paused, shielding their eyes against the glare. Dominic leant on the horn. We didn't need a second summons. Racing through the gate, we jumped into the open door and Dominic crashed the gears into reverse, lurched back into the road, and then, with another squeal of tyres, sped off down the street, leaving the vigilantes staring at our tail lights.

3. My Worst Enemy

The thought briefly occurred to me that she'd set this up on purpose just to make me homeless so I'd do whatever she wanted. Girls, I'd heard, can be devious like that.

I don't believe in luck, fate or destiny; they're all comfort words that humans have. It's just you, what you're like, that makes certain kinds of events happen to you rather than others. Me, I attract trouble cos I'm a hybrid. People like me give a new meaning to the word 'dysfunctional'.

This time, as Dominic drove, Kestrella told me more about herself. She was different from anyone I'd met before. She'd seen the world, met all kinds – except dregs like me – and grown up in the type of universe where people fly their own jet to their own private island in the sun for a four-day party attended by tycoons, politicians and actors. In such a world, nobody asks too many questions and everyone feels safe. She said even I would fit in – with the right clothes.

"A hybrid?" I said. "Aren't they afraid they might catch Something Nasty?"

She shook her head causing tangled black curls to wave around her face, and I began to think how beautiful it might be to run my hand through them. But that was a stupid thought.

"They think their wealth makes them immune from anything," she said.

"Didn't help you, did it? How come you're part of that set?"

"Maman. She used to be a top model. She is still the most beautiful person I've ever seen." Kestrella went silent for a moment and her lips curled inwards as if she was swallowing something that she didn't want to let free. "She was on the covers of glossy magazines and in the gossip columns."

I was wondering what to say when her phone rang. It was a slender model in the style popular a couple of years ago. The keypad was where her palm might have been and the screen was in place of her fingers. It was one of the most common types of rewrite. I filed a picture of it alongside the dozens of others I kept in a database.

I'd already sensed that the vehicle we were in had a built-in wireless satellite system, probably for her father's work given the nature of the passwords I'd picked my way through, and I uploaded the database on to a remote server. I'd actually not lost much except hardware from the attack on my place. I was always careful to copy my files on to several servers, sometimes splitting them up and distributing the pieces on servers across the world so that nobody picking up one of them would ever be able to tell what it was.

I'm not paranoid, just realistic, OK?

The 4x4 was passing through an area of old office blocks. A long section of hoarding was plastered with competing posters from different political parties for a public demonstration and counter-demonstration. Some read COMPULSORY QUARANTINE NOW! Others read PROTECTION NOT PERSECUTION.

At the next intersection, the car slowed down as it passed a Gene Police van and two patrol cars, recognisable from the logo on their sides: a DNA double helix snaking round a flaming torch. They had spilled out a dozen foot soldiers in their white, hermetically sealed suits, who were surrounding a scooter that had smashed into a lamp post. Only it wasn't just a scooter.

I could see a human face contorted in agony, and I'm sure that the driver's right hand somehow merged with the handlebars… I cringed inside: nothing could be done. The GP had probably spotted and given chase to their quarry, pushing him harder and harder through the city's back streets until he'd crashed.

Kestrella was talking in her light French accent to someone about being somewhere. She finished and turned to me with a fierce Gallic look in her eye. "This time you're not to argue. We're going back to Salvation House and you're going to meet my aunt Cheri, OK? Dominic?"

The red light flashing angrily on my screen bounced off the slight sheen of perspiration on her forehead. "You're not going to register me. I don't want to become a Blue like you. I'm a Grey and I intend to stay that way, got it?"

She smiled wryly. "You know something? I'm beginning to think you are your own worst enemy."

A statement like that left me cold. After all I had that block of ice to keep from melting. "I'd rather be free, don't you see?" I said defiantly. "I need to be free."

She laughed. "What good is freedom if your life is in danger, if you're in hiding and can't function properly?"

"You, you may be free to jet to your own island in the sun whenever you like," I threw back, "but you don't understand what freedom means, and you never will until you have people trying to take it away from you just because of what you are!"

"Ha! How romantic!" She threw her head back. "Your freedom is nothing if you can't make good use of it!"

I turned away from her, breathing heavily. Why was I so angry? I had nowhere to go, but why should that make me dependent on her and her aunt? I could find another place to be, couldn't I? I could break into another house and squat, as I had so many times before. There were clubs, cafés, dens I knew that could tolerate someone like me: they were part of the subculture.

My heart was pounding, I was hyperventilating and I could feel my transition points flaring up and feeling hot. There were—

The next thing I knew I was on the floor of the car, staring up into Kestrella's face – was that a tear in her eye? – writhing like a wounded animal at the pain down my left arm. Pain like a hot needle pushing down into my wrist, where the keyboard poked out – one of my transition points. She had pulled up my sleeve to see what it looked like and the expression of horror on her face made even me feel frightened. I don't know how long I'd blacked out for, but Dominic had stopped the car and he too was reaching over me, his mirror shades reflecting the white noise on my monitor.

He'd opened the fridge and got out a spray can of I-So-L8 and was spraying it on to the affected area. It felt cool. The soreness gradually faded away, the white noise went, a screensaver picture of one of my favourite bands now bounced off Dominic's shades as he pulled away from me and Kestrella breathed a sigh of relief, the tear gone.

She turned to Dominic: "Are we nearly there yet?" she said.

4. Salvation House

I always liked coming to Salvation House. The building itself was Victorian redbrick, but with a modern wing, all light, gleaming glass and potted plants. It seemed happy in spite of the suffering it held; it appeared to hold its darkness easily. This was due to the staff, who always tried to give their dependants hope that it was possible to get better and one day lead a normal life.

Of course, no one ever had.

But that didn't matter, it was the feeling that counted; that you were among people who cared. Many of the willing workers here were volunteers, and the hospice survived on grants and donations given by anyone who could get beyond the idea that hybrids should be feared or blamed for their condition. But there weren't many compared to those who did fear or blame them.

This place owed so much to the personality and drive of one woman: Cheri Dubois. She had been, from the time when she used to hoist me on to her knee and sing nursery rhymes, *ma tante* Cheri, my mother's elder sister.

She was now behind the door I was looking at, inside an examination room with a nurse and this obstinate boy who I'd finally managed to drag in here, but under a promise I wasn't sure I could keep.

They were inside for ages. I passed the time by having a cappuccino and a Danish pastry in the cafeteria in the leafy conservatory with Dominic and some of the regular drop-in visitors. They came to pick up medication, have a massage or a check-up. I read the adverts on the noticeboards, about campaign meetings, fundraising events, therapies such as herbalism or acupuncture, and pleas for supportive carers for newly registered sufferers, who needed a sponsor to avoid being sent to the dreaded Centre for Genetic Rehabilitation.

No one could stay in the hospice forever. Pressure on space was too great. Cheri had told me that last year they had 1300 people passing through their doors, but they only had beds for thirty-five at any one time. And it was getting worse.

I left Dominic in the café and wandered to the residential section in the quiet south wing where the smell was antiseptic. When I popped in on Julian, he was sitting up in bed looking as thin as a stick insect. He was sixteen and yet his skin was like brown paper stretched over chicken wire. His eyes were trying to hide deep in their sockets, but shone with electrical energy. His body seemed to hum like a generator.

"Kestrella darling! You look more beautiful than ever," he smiled weakly.

He let me kiss his gleaming forehead. He could read the expression on my face.

"I know I still look ill," he said, "but don't worry. I'm going to be fine. They say there's no cure for the pandemic. But I reckon I've found one."

"Really, Julian?" I said, sitting down.

He paused to sniff some sort of inhaler. "I've taken control of my life. I don't eat bad food any more. That's why I got ill before – you know. I treated my body like a rubbish bin. God, why did I hate it so much? I do my exercises. And I've become a Buddhist." I noticed, in a corner of the room, a low table with a statue and candles. "I meditate. I picture my body being healthy and fit. And it's working. Isn't it, Angie?"

His nurse, had entered the room. She smiled but gave me a knowing look.

"Well, you certainly look better than you did when

you came in and no mistake." Angie checked his pulse. I didn't know what the exact nature of his condition was – it wasn't polite to ask and he hadn't told me.

"I really hope it works, Julian. I'll be rooting for you."

"You were here yesterday. Has your aunt got you on the payroll?"

I laughed. "No, I've brought someone in. A rather special patient."

His eyebrows lifted and he tried to prop himself up on one elbow but failed. "Really? Do tell…"

I stood up. "Later, Julian. I have to be sure he survives the night first. I'll be back soon, OK? I just popped in to check on you." I pecked his forehead and smelt his aroma of stale apricots. "Take care now."

As I left, I bumped into a boy in the corridor. As soon as he saw me he blinked his eyes and opened his mouth. A roll of paper fed out along his tongue and a photograph materialised on it. He handed me the photo. "See you around," he said and walked off.

I looked at the picture. It was me: with a huge bleached out nose and rabbit eyes. Did I feel as scared as I looked?

I passed Maeve's room. She was a thirteen-year-old in a bed specially engineered to accommodate the electronic keyboard that extended from her arms and fingertips. She smiled weakly at me as a nurse gave her a painkiller.

I started as someone pounced on me from behind. "Hello, kid!" It was Cheri. Steel-grey bouquet of hair, piercing grey eyes, tall, and dressed in a new version of her customary blue linen trousers and matching jacket that I thought made her look like a cleaner. She took my arm and steered me down a well-lit corridor bustling with staff and visitors towards her office. "You've picked a right one there, haven't you?" she said.

"What do you mean? How's Johnny?" I asked.

"Asleep. We've put him in Elton John Ward. He's going to be in la-la land for a very long time if you ask me. Mon dieu, he's been living on the edge for so long he doesn't know which way is up."

"But will he be OK?"

"Not sure yet. He has multiple infections. We've put him on the standard course of antibiotics and Stabil-O-Gene. Now we wait for the test results to come in. Here." She ushered me into her office, which, although she was the director of the hospice, looked much like all the others. "Come and sit down. You look pretty wired yourself."

"I'm OK." Cheri's desk was covered with paperwork. Two monitors blinked. There were flowering plants.

"You picked him because…"

"Er…" I felt put on the spot. "He's unknown to the authorities and he appears to be a computer genius."

"And now you've met him?"

"He's… not what I expected. Younger, and more insecure than I thought."

"Yes. Will you still ask him?"

"Why? Do you think I shouldn't?"

Cheri pretended to sort through a few papers in a pile. "We agreed to do this, or rather I agreed to your suggestion. We've brought him in and now we are responsible for him."

I hadn't quite thought of it like that, but it was true. Before, Johnny was a free agent. Because of me his life had been changed forever. "But he couldn't have gone on living that way. He was lucky he wasn't at home when that gang attacked his room."

"Go home, darling," Cheri said tenderly. "Come back tomorrow. He'll sleep for eighteen hours at least."

I could tell I was being dismissed; the great director was busy.

"And not a word to your papa, OK?" she said. I hated it when she was still my aunt.

On the way out, I saw a Gene Police wagon parked round the corner. It followed our 4x4 as we headed back to Docklands. It gave up as we entered the gated area. Maybe it was just there for our protection.

But I doubted it.

5. Playing with the Rhinoceros

In this dream I'm being chased by a rhinoceros around my parents' garden. I don't know how old I am.

It begins after the rhinoceros and I have been together in the garden for a while. Suddenly the rhinoceros takes a dislike to me; I can see the change in its eyes. It fixes me with a stare that sees right through to the guilty core of my soul that I thought I was able to keep hidden from everybody. But with its single horn it has successfully probed through my layers of protection, torn the veils of illusion I carefully hung up, tossed aside the blankets of lies I've spread and pierced the many masks of normalcy I've spent years laying down. And it's done this so casually and quickly that I'm defenceless.

So the rhinoceros is charging at me and I'm looking around for somewhere to avoid it. I dodge round the pampas grass and the yucca plant, still in flower, but my muscles are damaged and I can't jump or somersault over the wall. I forget the narrow passage down the side of the house through which I could escape since it's too tight for the rhinoceros. I fail to spot the rain butt and how I could leap on it and shin up the drainpipe on to the roof of the rear extension. And so I'm powerless to escape from the path of the charging rhinoceros with its unblinking eyes permanently locked on to mine.

This being a dream, the rhinoceros never impacts upon me. I never feel the splintering contact of the first or even the second horn.

Instead, just before the moment of connection, the dream cuts back as if in a loop to the beginning, and here I am hanging out with the rhinoceros again, in the same garden, on the suburban lawn, with the low wall and the pampas and yucca. But this time I know that the rhinoceros is soon going to realise how guilty I am deep inside, and then bristle with immense dislike, work up a head of steam beneath the metallic sheen of its armoured hide and finally launch its attack. Again, I am completely unable to do anything about it.

There's that look in its eyes again, that timeless stare of cold hatred and judgement, a moment strung out for eternity when we both know what's going to happen next. But I can't move until the rhinoceros moves, and then it does, and I'm trying to make my body work, but it won't, limping, tumbling over the low wall, falling to the right. None of it works, the rhinoceros looms larger and larger and...

Back to square one again.

This time it's just the same, but I'm aware of the house, my home, the blank windows staring at the garden, at me, but seeing nothing. Is nobody inside the house? Why don't they notice what's happening? Why doesn't anybody come out and save me? Anyway, where does the rhinoceros come from? Does it belong to us? Have my parents bought it as a pet? Or has it in fact sprung from within my own mind, this being why it knows me so well?

There's no time to think. It has that look in its eyes again. Oh well, here it comes: the pantomime chase like an old silent comedy. And the point of the horn heading for me but never quite making it because...

The two of us. The garden. The pampas grass and the yucca. The high hedges and fences all around to stop the prying eyes of neighbours. I look at you, for you are the rhinoceros and the rhinoceros is me, looking at me. The two of us stare at each other, knowing everything there is to know about anything, especially about me. And then you charge, or I charge, and really, then, I realise that this is why it's happening.

The rhinoceros, with its two probing, mineral horns and iron hide, its composite organic/inorganic form, transformed into a monster of hate, and I, we are the same thing. We absolutely deserve to have become each other, in the absence of any onlookers to save us, and to feel the guilt we hold. Together we are me and my non-human, electronic, plastic, silicon and copper parts. My nanochips, my digital parasite, my rhinoceros.

And slowly I wake up.

6. The Mother of all Missions

I wasn't there when he woke up, but Cheri called me at home and, as I wasn't far away, I said I'd be there in half an hour.

It was a Sunday. The streets of London were even less crowded now that most of the shops had closed down. The pandemic had changed everything.

But I was trying to put aside my cares. I told myself I must see Johnny as a separate person from my need, with his own worries and concerns. If I pushed too hard, I would lose the possibility of his help.

The fact that Johnny had no eyes or mouth, and no voice of his own, only a computer-generated one, made it hard to know what he felt. The only clue was whatever he chose to display on his monitor. When I entered, it was showing a slow-moving animation of abstract images. Relaxing music – was he singing? – was seeping from his speakers and swirling around the room. I took this to mean he was feeling better.

Angie was adjusting his pillow. She smiled at me and left the room. When Johnny spoke, his voice was different from before: higher, softer… but still abrupt and without the preamble of a greeting.

"When can I leave?"

"I don't know," I said. "It's not up to me. Don't you like it here?"

"It's OK." He shrugged. "They gave me this leaflet." He held it up: a brochure explaining all the facilities at Salvation House. "Shall I read this part to you? 'All patients, whether attending on a daily or drop-in basis, or residential, must be registered with the Home Office.'" His camera fixed me with its unwavering stare.

"Yes. Well, that's because they'd close this place down otherwise, wouldn't they?" I looked at my hand and phone.

"You promised I wouldn't be registered."

"As far as I know you haven't been," I said tightly. "Do you feel better now?"

He turned away. "A little. But I had a weird dream."

I sat next to the bed and handed him the carnations I'd brought. He mumbled some thank-you words; perhaps no one had given him flowers before. As he took them, the sleeve of his hospital gown slipped back to reveal more points where bits of a keyboard seemed to protrude from his lower inside arm. I couldn't help staring – it looked horribly inflamed and bruised and I'd never seen anything like it. The sleeve quickly slipped down again and I looked directly at the small camera embedded in his forehead like a third eye. Beneath it his pixels formed a smiley face. Perhaps that was Johnny's way of saying thank you for the flowers, but it betrayed nothing of the pain or discomfort I knew he must feel.

"I have a question. Why are you helping me?"

I took a deep breath. "You know how I found you on the Internet and read your blog. There's your manifesto, isn't there?"

"'Declaration of the Rights of Hybrids', yes."

"It's really good. Everybody's talking about it."

"Really? I just did it so I wouldn't feel so alone. I mean, it's fairly obvious stuff."

"Cheri likes it. The trustees have got it pinned up in the foyer. They hold debates here. But I don't know if I can do anything brave like you," I said.

"When your back's against the wall and you've got nothing to lose it doesn't seem brave. It seems the only thing to do."

"You give examples. Things people can do. Like…

refusing to co-operate with the Gene Police. Not registering hybrids…"

Johnny was sitting up now, clearly animated. "Hacking medical companies' files, disabling government databases."

"Yes. Tell me, have you done that yourself?"

There was a pause while his screen went still. "Maybe I have, maybe I haven't." I understood that he didn't want to incriminate himself. "But you still haven't told me why you wanted to meet," he said.

"That's kind of why. It's about Maman."

"Your mother?"

I nodded. "Three months ago she caught Creep, probably from me though she said not."

His monitor screen stopped swirling so fast and turned to a blue scene. "I'm sorry."

"Papa thought she could be cared for at home like me, but hadn't got around to registering her yet. She was still a Grey. But then—"

"She disappeared. One day. Just like that. While out somewhere," Johnny interrupted, question marks flashing on his screen.

I stared at him. "How did you know?"

"'S common. Sometimes people're picked up by the GP, other times…"

"…Vigilantes." There was silence for a moment. "I know. It's what I'm most afraid of."

"When did she vanish?" he asked.

"Ten days ago. We've tried everything to find her. Oh, Johnny, I'm getting so desperate. I miss her so much. You must know how I feel…"

"I don't think my situation's quite the same as yours," he intoned.

"What do you mean?"

"I came home from school one day and my parents weren't there," he said in a low voice.

"Just like that?"

"Uh-huh."

"You mean they'd left you?"

"Moved out. Clothes, furniture, everything. Didn't bother to tell me where to, did they? Why should they? I'm a hybrid. Unwanted."

I was struck dumb as I absorbed the enormity of this betrayal.

"What did you do?"

"Went wandering."

"Didn't you try to find them?"

"What on earth for? Look, I don't want to talk about it, all right?" he snapped. "Just tell me what you want from me."

"Could you help find my mother? You're good at hacking and things. Johnny, I must know if she's alive or not. Cheri's her sister. She agreed to help me. We'll do anything we can in return. What do you say?"

At that moment Cheri herself came in carrying a clipboard. She was wearing exactly the same as yesterday: had she been to bed at all?

"Ah." She came over to check the records at the bottom of his Johnny's bed. "How's the sleepy patient today, mmm? Do we have any results?"

The ward sister who had followed her in handed her a printout. "Blood test: RTGV positive − version 4b. Low on iron and red blood cells. Infections easing but not clear yet."

"Thanks, Jenny. Hmm." Cheri studied the test results, then fixed Johnny with a gaze. "I'm afraid this means we're going to have to keep you here a few days. You're not seriously ill from the secondary infections, but you could be if you go out too soon and continue your old way of life."

"I thought I'd been looking after myself all right," he said, sounding petulant, and more like the fifteen-year-old that he was. I realised that his artificial voice and height made him seem older.

"Actually, you've been having very poor nutrition. So

your immune system is low and you've developed mild blood poisoning, chronic inflammation at the organic-inorganic interfaces and anaemia. You're basically susceptible to any virus or infection going around."

His screen shut down for a moment.

Cheri turned to me. "So… No stress, OK? You haven't been bothering the patient, have you, Kestrella?"

There she was, pulling the Responsible Aunt thing on me again. "I only asked him what we agreed I would, Auntie," I said, in as level a voice as I could manage.

"Oh, you did, did you?" Cheri studied Johnny. "You were supposed to wait a few days, child."

"But we can't wait any longer!" I cried. "Every day means— Maman might be— Anything could happen to her."

"Yes, but that is not this boy's affair, is it? What did he say?"

"Nothing yet."

We both looked at him. He'd turned his body away from us.

"Then I think we should let him think about it for a few days, don't you?"

"But Aunt Cheri!" I pleaded.

"We'll not stand a chance if our patient gets worse, will we, darling?" she said with finality.

I felt powerless and exasperated. After all I'd done. But then the patient spoke.

"I can begin from here," he said. "There's wi-fi in the building."

I looked at Johnny with grateful disbelief. He'd said yes! He wanted to help me! I felt so happy. But then…

"No, I'm sorry. It will tire you. What you need now is rest," said Cheri.

"But Auntie—" I begged.

"Do you want to kill him?" she said.

"I can be the judge of that," Johnny said. "But before I agree to help there's one thing I need to ask you first. You're in charge here, aren't you?" Cheri nodded.

Without the slightest trembling of his hand or adjustment in posture he spoke in his near monotone to Cheri: "Did you register me?"

Cheri adjusted her posture to its full height. She said in her firm, professional voice: "By law, every hybrid we treat has to be registered. Failure to do so, and to find a responsible carer for them, means they have to be taken to the Centre for Genetic Rehabilitation, which is run by the government."

I could feel the anger welling up inside him from where I stood.

Cheri continued. "The Gene Police already know you exist because they monitor all our patients. You can bet your last chromosome that if you left here unregistered they wouldn't rest till they'd picked you up."

There was a short silence during which Johnny didn't move, but I could sense the stiffening of his body and the churning of unseen circuits. Then he emitted a huge roar. A brilliant light from his screen threw everything into relief and suddenly all the bulbs in the room went out. The humming of machines that I hadn't noticed before ceased abruptly, to reveal a horrible silence. The only illumination came from the street outside through the window blinds. The silence and darkness were all the more effective after the roar and brightness beforehand. Nobody said anything for – I swear – ten seconds, but I fought to keep my panic down. Finally Cheri spoke, her voice soft and calm.

"Johnny, did you do that?"

But he didn't reply.

Then, from somewhere within the bowels of the building, an emergency generator kicked in and lights flickered back on; the humming coughed a bit and resumed, and little whirrings woke up to begin their work all over again. We looked at the bed.

It was empty.

7. The Rifle Man

Didn't it just go to show how you can't trust anybody?

Take my mother: I could never trust her with my secrets. Take my father: you could only trust him to write a report or something like that. But to take you to the cinema when he said he would? The only thing he seemed to care about was his work. Eventually, they stopped pretending to take responsibility for me, setting an example for everyone else to follow. And to cap it all, for the past three years the electronic world has been just as unreliable. Why should this girl and her aunt be any different?

Running down a corridor, I found a fire exit at the back of the hospice. It led into a utility yard from which a dark passage struck off around the side. At the end was a stiff iron gate which I managed to climb over. I heard the shouting first. What I saw next stopped me in my tracks. On the pavement in front of the hospice a small crowd had gathered, and they hadn't come to bring flowers to the patients inside.

"Quarantine now! Quarantine now!"

Led by a tall, middle-aged man in a suit wielding a megaphone, they were waving placards with slogans such as: "Close Salvation House!", "Hybrids are not human", "Protect the human race" and "Keep Britain normal!"

I shrank into a dark corner next to the gate where I could see what was going on.

The crowd was about thirty-strong. As they realised they had no opposition, they grew bolder, their chanting louder, and they began to rattle sticks against the railings. A security guard stood inside his hut next to the vehicle barrier, which was down. He was talking into his radio and looking worried. Some of the crowd was ready to dodge underneath the barrier, but the rest hadn't plucked up enough courage yet. Another guard ran out to join the first and stood on the other side of the barrier facing the protesters. They didn't look like they would be able to put up much of a fight.

Where were the Gene Police? They were never there when you wanted them.

They weren't really called the Gene Police. Officially known as the Biological Security Force, their job was to round up Greys. They also had a security role so they should be here, keeping the peace. But they weren't, and that, for me, confirmed what I'd heard about them. This mob was doing what the authorities secretly wanted to, but couldn't.

There was nothing for me to do but stay where I was and sit it out. After a few minutes the man with a megaphone turned to address the crowd, but the wind carried his words away. My camera could zoom in on him though – greying beard, anorak over old grey suit, baseball cap, tall as a post. I took pictures of him and everybody I could see in the crowd – you never knew when they'd be useful. Now the group surged forward, dodging around and under the barrier.

The guards put up little resistance. Salvation House was set on a quiet side street with little traffic at this time. No one was going to intervene.

"Hybrids out! Hybrids out!" echoed off the walls.

The crowd was now in the forecourt and had begun to pick up bricks from a pile of builders' rubble. The megaphone man threw the first one. I heard the sound of breaking glass, a shriek from inside, and hoped nobody had been hit. I imagined Cheri and Kestrella hustling all the patients to cover.

Soon missiles were raining through several windows at the front, the rhythm of the chanting broken down into random shouts. Someone lit a petrol bomb. But before they could throw it, the almost gentle sound of breaking glass was cut through by a loud spray of automatic gunfire. It raked the ground in front of them, the noise tearing through the evening.

The shooter was hidden from my view. But the demonstrators turned to see where it had come from and I saw their reaction. The man holding the petrol bomb was panicking – he didn't know what to do with it. Before it could explode in his hand, he hurled it at the stone wall of the hospice. This prompted another burst of machine-gun fire and he howled as it strafed across his feet. The courage of the demonstrators evaporated like wet footprints in the midday sun. They turned and ran as fast as they could.

Now the shooter entered my frame of vision – a tall man in battle fatigues and, seen in silhouette, his right arm seemed to be an assault rifle. The two security guards came warily up to join him as the crowd vanished behind the barrier. All three stared down at the petrol bomber, who was whimpering and nursing his foot.

I began to think it might be safe to come out. But the evening's trouble wasn't over yet. The familiar Gene Police sirens were approaching – after all the violence was over. Three vans drew up by the barrier. Instead of the whole squad of officers pouring out of the vans as they usually did, just one man stepped down.

"Do you know who that is?" whispered a familiar voice behind me.

Startled, I turned round. I hadn't heard anyone approach.

"It's Major Malcolm Winter, the commander-in-chief of the Gene Police," said Kestrella.

"I recognise him, though I've never seen him in person before," I replied at my lowest volume.

"I was afraid the mob had got you," she said, and I noted the tender concern in her voice.

Winter was talking to the security guards, but the man with the rifle had mysteriously disappeared. Cheri came out and ran over to join them, clearly angry. It seemed as if she knew Winter. They began to argue, arms waving about.

"Come back inside with me." Kestrella brushed her mobile phone against the palm of my hand through the gate's bars. It felt warm. "I know you're angry, but you can't leave now, not with them there. Besides, there are a few other things, very important things, which you need to know."

I turned to face her. Her long hair was being blown

around her face in the cool evening air and she met my gaze steadily.

"You let me down. You said I wouldn't be registered."

"Don't be so quick to judge," she said. "You know, for a boy who's half computer, you're not at all logical. Are you?"

I'd never thought of that before. I thought I was completely logical. Anybody in my position would do what I'd done.

Wouldn't you?

8. Papa

It was ten in the evening and Dominic was driving us through the City of London. The financial district was empty of people, normal or hybrid. Many windows were boarded up – they couldn't rent out office space since the rest of the world threw a quarantine order round Britain. Other countries were desperate to prevent the disease spreading out of the UK. As a result, the UK economy had collapsed, with millions of unemployed people stuck in their homes, afraid to venture forth.

I was taking Johnny to my home – and he didn't seem to like it. I could feel the aura of anxiety around him. Whenever I tried to reassure him, he flinched away.

I understood why my aunt had to register him; she had a difficult job. She worked so hard keeping the hospice together and could only do that if she followed certain rules set by the government. We eventually helped Johnny see that being registered did carry certain advantages. Although the authorities had to know where you were all the time, you could go anywhere, almost, as long as you were tagged and under the authority of a responsible "normal" person. I guess because she felt responsible for Johnny being there, Cheri volunteered for this role. As we were to discover, this was not a good idea.

I looked at Johnny: was he sulking, tired or sick? It was hard to tell. On his screen was a picture of a monkey in a cage. It was asleep. He kept scratching his ankle where his new tag rubbed against his skin. Mine had been like that when I first got it. I'd hated it. I was used to it now.

"I can see why it's called Creep," I said. "I used to think it was just because metal, plastic and minerals were gradually taking over the living parts of human beings. But now I can see how it's got to do with the way a plague creeps like a stain through a healthy population."

"Yeah," he grunted. "Creepy, isn't it?"

Now we were approaching a high-density enclave of luxury offices, apartments and shops on the estuary side, north of the river. This was where I lived with my father and other rich people. Johnny sat up and took notice now. He'd never been here before. As we approached the security gates, Dominic triggered the infra-red signal and let us in, watched by a battery of CCTV cameras. I breathed a sigh of relief even though I knew it was completely irrational. I was really no safer on this side than on the other. If I had been, I would obviously never have got ill.

I felt faint. It was time for my medication and I didn't have any more with me. I couldn't wait to get to the fridge, smooth the I-So-L8 cream over my burning skin and feel its magic working into my chromosomes. "Correcting fluid" Papa called it. We parked in the multi-storey and took the lift to the 30th.

All the way sensors scanned our irises – except for Johnny who didn't have any. I wondered what the machines thought about that.

"Listen, I think it's better not to let Sim know that Johnny wrote the Declaration of the Rights of Hybrids," said Cheri as we walked up the corridor to the apartment door.

"Why?" asked Johnny.

"Because he might not want you under his roof if he knew, of course!"

"You mean he'd have heard about it?" asked Johnny.

"Of course!"

The door opened and Cheri took Johnny into the living room while I rushed to the fridge. Soon my soreness began to wear off and I felt more normal.

"So this is where you live." Johnny was standing by the window looking at the incredible view. The lights of London spread out like an inversion of a starry night, a spangled carpet of white and orange dots already joined into constellations by streetlights. The moving lights of traffic were like UFOs journeying between galaxies. Through it all, a big black snake lying bloated and growing by the year – the river, which would one day swallow half the city.

"Not bad," he said. "I bet it costs more to live here in a year than most people earn in a lifetime."

"You bet it does," growled a familiar voice. I turned around to see Papa enter from the hallway and throw his briefcase on to a chair. Evidently he had just arrived from the office. I ran to him and buried my head in his chest. I needed to feel closer to him ever since Maman had disappeared.

"You've been gone a long time, Papa," I murmured. I felt his pepper-and-salt bristle tickle my cheek, but perhaps he didn't like the suggestion that he was neglecting me because he got up to fix himself a drink.

"Somebody has to do the work. And this place doesn't pay for itself." He looked tired, his Oriental skin paler than usual.

"Any news?" I asked hopefully, as I had every day since she'd gone, though I could tell the answer from his face.

He shook his head. "No, darling. Not yet."

"Hello, Sim," said Cheri to draw attention to herself.

"Ah, it's the bleeding-heart liberal. Good evening." He prepared a gin and tonic. "What brings you here? Have you found your sister? And who is this boy?" He turned to face Johnny. "I take it he's registered?"

He started to inspect Johnny as if he were an exhibit in a museum and I began to feel irritated. Ever since Maman disappeared he'd begun to drink more and I didn't like it. It seemed to bring out the worst in him.

"You don't need to worry about breaking the law," said Cheri. The government had recently made it illegal for anyone to host a Grey on their property. "He's mine."

Johnny had generated a smiley face. I already knew him well enough to understand that this meant he was being polite.

"Computer type," Papa said, peering closely at the transition points. "Never seen one quite as advanced as this."

Immediately the smiley face changed to a frowny one. "It's all right," spoke his impersonal, electronic voice. "You don't have to be polite with me. After all, I'm no longer human."

"So sorry," said Papa. "Just that in my line of work…" and his voice trailed off.

"That's right, make a complete fool of yourself," said my aunt. "This is Johnny. Your daughter brought him to Sally House."

"Hm," Papa smiled. "Can you roll up your sleeve?" He inspected the surface of Johnny's arm where parts of the keyboard protruded. "Very interesting. Multiple interfaces. Unusual specimen."

Curiously, Johnny didn't seem to mind this scrutiny.

Papa stood back. "OK. How do you eat and breathe, Johnny?"

Stiffly, Johnny showed him the feed bottle and tubes that entered his throat and oesophagus. At the moment the bottle was half full of coffee.

"I should explain, Johnny," said Cheri. "Sim Chu is in charge of media relations and marketing at Mu-Tech, the biotech corporation. He therefore has a professional interest in your condition."

"I know," said Johnny and addressed him directly. "It's your job to come up with promotional campaigns for products like Stabil-O-Gene, Gene-U-Like and I-So-L8, isn't it?"

"Correct," said Papa, with a hint of pride in his voice.

"… all those quack snake oils with horrendous side-effects. You play on the fear of normal people of catching the disease, exploiting their paranoia to make money for your shareholders." Johnny's artificial voice delivered this in a level, matter-of-fact way. I watched Papa carefully. He didn't blink for a moment.

"Well, it's a very real fear," he smiled benignly. "Isn't everyone afraid? Of course. Especially because nobody knows how the virus is transmitted. I know the drugs we have aren't so good yet. When we understand the cause we'll have a better chance to come up with the cure. Until then I'm afraid these drugs are the best we can do."

"There's a rumour companies like yours came up with the disease in the first place and let it loose on the population just so you could sell them the medicines." Johnny wasn't pulling any punches.

"I'm aware of this rumour," said Papa, sitting down and making himself comfortable. "But it is not true. You are very young, Johnny, and don't have much experience yet, therefore it is understandable you might believe such conspiracy theories. And yet do you think I would continue to work for this company if it had really done that, when two members of my own family are suffering from the disease?"

Johnny sat down as well, on a long white sofa opposite my father. "I said it got out of hand. Once you let the genie out of the bottle, or the genes out of the lab, you have no control over what'll happen. I bet nobody ever meant it to get to this stage."

"No, that's not so. Johnny, you've had a hard time in your short life. And you are looking for someone to blame. But it's not me or my company. I hope in time, as a friend of my daughter's, you will come to see Mu-Tech as part of the solution not part of the problem."

I went to sit next to Papa on the arm of his chair and let him put his arm around my waist. We both stared across the room at Johnny. Now Sim was stroking my wrist where it turned into the mobile phone. "You know I'd give my right arm today if my daughter could get her hand back and I could get my wife back."

"Which brings me to the reason why he's here, Papa," I said.

"Oh yes, darling?" He looked at me expectantly.

"Johnny, you see, is a computer head. In more senses than one. He's brilliant on the Internet. He's agreed to help me look for Maman."

"Well," said Papa. "If you think you can do better than the police and emergency forces, don't let me stop you." He was being sarcastic again and withdrew his arm from my waist. "I told you before this idea is ridiculous. And I am surprised at you, Cheri, encouraging my daughter with such silly ideas. Didn't I tell you I already got a private detective on the case at great expense?"

"But Papa, you just said you'd give your right arm to get her back. What have we got to lose?"

"Your sanity? Who knows? Oh," he lifted my leg off his knee and got up. "Do what you like, girl – you always do anyway. Now, if you don't mind, I must go to bed. I have a meeting at seven o'clock tomorrow. Where is Dominic?"

"I think he's in his room. Probably reading," I said.

"Very good. Well, so sorry but I am very tired. Goodnight everyone."

He pecked my cheek semi-automatically and wandered into his part of the apartment. I stared at Johnny and Cheri. It was Cheri who spoke first. "It's the stress. Got to be. I don't think he used to be as bad as this. Kestrella, don't take it personally. Inside, he must be as worried as we are, and if he does have a private eye working for him, so much the better."

"Yes," agreed Johnny. "And three heads are better than one, especially if one of them is mine. Tomorrow, we'll get to work."

For the first time in the ten days since Maman disappeared, I began to feel just a little bit of hope.

9. The Mendel Arms

Before Creep ended my childhood, I used to think life should be fair. Isn't it weird how kids think that?

After Creep, I knew it wasn't fair. So I started believing life was random – like the chance mutations that cause evolution. There was no point to anything at all.

But suppose I was wrong? Then there'd be a reason why Creep had got me. In my darker moments I thought I must have done something awful to deserve it and this was my punishment. Sometimes I thought it had given me special abilities to help me achieve something great. Maybe, just maybe, finding Kestrella's mum was it.

Kestrella gave me a bed in a spare room where everything was white, including the thick duvet on the double bed and the long woollen curtains. It was like being in a cloud. Kestrella and Cheri slept somewhere else.

After a few hours' sleep, Sim went off to work. He'd gone by the time we got up.

Over breakfast Cheri showed me a photograph. There was a lot of Kestrella in her mother's face, but it was like a mask, made inscrutable with practice. She gazed blankly out of the photo like someone completely bored with life. But as she was a model, she was probably just bored with cameras. Her closely cropped blonde hair emphasised her high forehead, the large, deep pools of her blue eyes, the high cheekbones and red lips pouting from habit.

When I asked what type of hybrid she was, they told me Jacquelyn wouldn't say.

"She was coy about it," said Kestrella.

"There was no obvious difference in her appearance," said Cheri. "And, you know, one doesn't ask..."

"But you're her sister!" I protested. "Surely she would have told you." I saw a glance pass between her and Kestrella, but I couldn't tell what it meant.

"She didn't see fit to confide in me," explained Cheri. "She said she was seeing a private doctor. But we don't know who it was. Now, if you're going to search, you need to know that she had two surnames: her married name, Chu, and our name, which was also her professional name – Dubois."

"Are you still Dubois?" I asked Cheri.

She nodded. "Too busy to marry!" she said.

Cheri left after breakfast, making me promise on no account to go out till she came back. I began a web search. There were millions of references to Jacquelyn as a model and as a charity worker to filter out. As I expected, the most common search engines revealed nothing. The family would already have tried that themselves.

Cheri had suggested I look for people recently taken into police custody or hospital. Kestrella said, "We already tried to find out by phoning the hospitals and police stations, but turned up nothing."

So I turned to trying to hack into their systems. I decided to check all the hospitals, the police stations and Gene Police HQs in the surrounding fifty mile radius. That took all day. For lunch and supper Kestrella fed me liquidised soup with chicken and real vegetables, and more smoothies. The work and good food made me tired. By the evening I'd given up.

"Sorry, Kestrella, the ones I can get into, she's not there. The others are shutting me out."

Kestrella looked at me in a way I liked, a mixture of gratitude, concern and hope. She phoned Cheri at Salvation House, who asked to speak to me.

"I thought that might happen," she said. "I'm going to introduce you to a friend. His name's Mark Jarrett and he's a TV journalist. Don't worry, he's on our side. He's got a small production company that makes current affairs programmes. Wait there till I come off duty then I'll take you to meet him."

To pass the time I let Kestrella use me as her personal jukebox and play some of the hundreds of hours of music stored in my system. I was surprised to find out we liked the same sort of music... Venus and the Blue Genes, Ghost in the Machine, and the Nanosplicers' *Naked in the Gene Pool*.

And we talked. I wasn't used to talking. I didn't like it: it made me think and feel things I didn't want to. She tried asking me about my parents. I told her I didn't know where they were. She said she couldn't believe parents could abandon their child like that. I changed the subject and she started talking about her mother.

"The last time I saw her was that morning at the breakfast table when she gave me my freshly squeezed orange juice. Because she wasn't registered she hated being shut up in the apartment like a caged animal. In the evening we came back and she wasn't there. She must have gone out on her own."

I said, "The more I know about her the better. What kind of person was she?"

"She could be really nice one minute and the next…" Kestrella sliced her hand through the air. "She hated being judged by her appearance. She hated being judged at all. Zut!" She slapped her hand to her mouth suddenly. "Why am I talking about her in the past tense! It's terrible!"

She grabbed hold of my hand and stared right at me as if she could see into my eyes. I found this very uncanny. "Johnny, she is going to come back. Isn't she?"

I didn't know what to say. Tears were running down her beautiful cheeks.

"Don't worry, Kestrella. If she can be found, I'll find her. I promise," I found myself saying as I patted her hand awkwardly.

She gulped, blew her nose and wiped her eyes, then continued. "She started a charity. She thought of all the models with addictions that she knew, with eating disorders and drug problems. She'd lost two friends to crack cocaine. A support line specially for young ones seemed like a good idea. What was your mum like?" she said suddenly.

"It doesn't matter," I said, annoyed. "I know you miss your mother, OK? But that doesn't mean I miss mine.

You like to remember your mother. I try to forget mine."

Kestrella frowned. "So what would you say if you met her again?"

I'd thought about it before. I'd run no end of fantasies in my mind about what I would do if I ran into her, like, turning a corner on a street, or looking through a shop window and there she was, or if she just turned up at my door. I'd imagined all kinds of scenarios, all kinds of reactions. I finally said: "I'd ignore her." It was the worst thing I could think of.

Cheri arrived and got Dominic to drive us to a pub in the East End of London. It was tucked away on a dark and uncleaned side street. The pub sign hanging outside showed a bespectacled man with receding hair, wearing a nineteenth-century monk's habit, clasping his arms across his chest. I noticed that one arm was considerably longer than the other. The name on the sign was *The Mendel Arms*.

It was dark inside. As usual I had my hoodie pulled over my head and nobody gave us a second glance as we walked through to the back. There, sitting at a table by himself, was a thirty-something man with a shock of brown hair, brown eyes, freckles and a rollneck pullover. He had the appearance of someone used to sleeping standing up. Mark Jarrett shook my hand vigorously and said he was very pleased to see me and that the name of his company was 3x+y Productions. From that I was able to dig up a list of their TV programmes – mostly stuff to do with politics and current affairs or international issues – not a comedy among them.

"I'm compiling material for a programme about the plague. I think there's more going on than the government is telling us," he announced.

"Like what?" I said.

"Well, you know the Prime Minister, Lionel Smith? Don't you think it strange he hasn't been seen in public for four months?"

"Yes," said Cheri, sipping her juice. "They say it's due to security reasons, but he hasn't even been on TV. A bit unusual for a politician, don't you think?"

Mark continued: "They've given the Gene Police new powers to arrest and detain anybody they suspect might not only be carrying the virus but also protesting against the way the government is dealing with the pandemic."

"And," added Cheri breathlessly, "it's becoming harder and harder for Salvation House to get the drugs we need. The drug companies keep putting the prices up."

"Somebody is making a lot of money out of this. And we're trying to uncover whether any of the politicians have shares in the drug companies."

I was beginning to get bored. I was obviously surrounded by people who thought the world should be fair and liked to complain when they discovered it wasn't. Personally, I thought they enjoyed complaining. I put up on my screen a crying smiley. Boo hoo.

The message sank in, so they finally got to the point. "And then," Mark said, "there's the Centre for Genetic Rehabilitation. That's where all the Reds get taken. And nobody knows what happens to them. It's covered by the Official Secrets Act. They're never seen again."

"Of course, the message is that they're all well taken care of. They have to go somewhere because they have nobody to take care of them in the outside world," said Cheri. "We can't take everybody."

"But if it's all hunky-dory, why won't they let me in with my camera to film it?" asked Mark. "I think it's because they use the hybrids illegally, attempting to find a cure."

Cheri left the table for a moment, to visit the toilet. While she was absent, Mark leant conspiratorially across the table at me.

"You know what?" he said. "I think Kestrella's mother is in the CGR. Don't you?"

I shrugged. "Could be. But I bet you want me to see if I can find out."

Mark said: "We could do it together. If you ask me, it's the most likely place for her to be."

10. Bearing Witness

You'd have thought Johnny would have wanted to live in my apartment, with every comfort he could need. But Cheri said he'd better live with her as she was his registered carer. So she put him in her tiny spare room. This made sense and I tried not to show I was disappointed, because I was beginning to like him and wanted to get to know him better. He might be weird, socially inept and frequently come out with the most bizarre stuff, but he was kind, brave, fascinating – and funny too, in an offbeat way.

His new room was small and poky, but he said he didn't mind. It only had a small window, but he said he was used to that. It was bare, with no paintings or tapestries on the wall as in our place, but Johnny said that gave him more space to let his mind wander.

Then there was the problem of his electronic tag.

How could he do any investigative work without Cheri being with him and with a tag on his leg? The Gene Police would be on him in five minutes and we'd never see him again. The tags are attuned to your body rhythm so even if he did manage to get one of them off, if it stopped detecting his body it would immediately send out a radio alarm. It worked by broadcasting a regular signal every thirty seconds and if that stopped, they'd also be knocking on your door before you could say reverse transpose genetic engineering, so you couldn't just break it.

Johnny had a solution: "All I have to do is create a duplicate of the signal and broadcast that from my room, and meanwhile deactivate my own tag so I can leave undetected."

It sounded easy when put like that.

I spent the hours watching Johnny at work. After a while I became used to his appearance and stopped being bothered by the way his screen was a shifting mask fused to his head. I began noticing other things about him instead. How delicate his long, nimble fingers were. How patient he was, that he would spend an hour carefully filing a piece of metal to just the right shape to fit in its place. How his angular, tall skeleton, which carried little flesh, still moved with a kind of grace. His long arms hung from his broad shoulders, always gently poised for action, and were continually being called to brush his long brown hair behind his ears.

I found myself wondering what his face had looked like before the rewrite took over. Did he have high cheekbones, a shy smile, twinkling eyes? Were his eyelashes long? Were his lips thin, or full and generous? And what colour were his eyes; warm and brown, or blue and piercing?

"Do you have any photos of what you used to look like?" I asked.

"Definitely not," he replied. "Why would I want to keep those? I'm no longer that person."

"But what did your face look like?" I persisted.

"It doesn't matter. Why do you want to know?"

"No reason," I said. "Just wondered…"

Whenever he was concentrating hard, he would forget to control what was on his screen and across it would flicker, often at incredible speed, an apparently random series of images and words. I liked that. It was like a glimpse into his mind. As the hours turned to days, I became fascinated by how some images would repeat… snatches of video of a room full of young teenagers laughing and cheering at the camera; a house with a sheet hanging out of an upstairs

window bearing the slogan "Hybrids Here to Stay!";
children playing; a cat washing itself; a Gene Police van
rushing by filmed through a bush. I didn't ask him
about any of it. It was a glimpse into another world –
his world.

After four days Johnny announced that his gadget was
complete.

"However, there's one problem," he said.

"Another one?" I said.

"I've got to test this first, before we can use it." He
held up the gadget: a metal box with an aerial, a switch
and a light. "If I switch it on and it works, then whoever
is monitoring it will receive two signals. So they'll be
suspicious. But if I deactivate the tag and this gadget
doesn't work, then they won't get a signal at all. Basically,
it's got to work first time or we're skewered."

"I see. So what shall we do?" I said.

"No problem," said Mark who had just entered the
room. "I can test it in the studio at work. It's got a metal
cage around it to block out radio interference."

"Brilliant!" said Johnny, handing him the box. "Go for
it. I'm sorry I can't come with you."

"I'll be right back," Mark said.

While we were waiting, we co-operated on preparing
a meal – Johnny was happy to help me right from the

first time he saw how hard it was for me to do many common tasks.

"Three hands are better than one," he joked as he helped me chop some vegetables and apples for soup, and grate some cheese.

"I wish I could be your eyes and nose too," I said.

As we ate, he sat opposite, playing for me on his screen silly cartoons he'd downloaded from the Internet. I laughed so hard I spattered soup all over the table.

When Mark returned after two hours it was with a smile on his face and we knew it had worked. "Are we ready for the moment of truth?" he said.

"Good a time as any," said Johnny.

The tag sent out a signal once every thirty seconds, so that was how long they had to deactivate it and activate the gadget. Johnny didn't want to break it and take it off his leg because he might have to show it to somebody sometime. He had simply to remove the tiny battery at the right time, which it was possible to do with a Torx screwdriver.

I held a stopwatch. Johnny removed the battery. I immediately started counting down from thirty. On "one" Mark switched on the fake. There was a moment when we thought it hadn't worked but then the little box let out a beep. We breathed a sigh of relief and I jumped up and down.

"Well, Johnny, I guess this means you're a free man again," said Mark.

I nearly hugged Johnny, but if he was pleased he didn't show it. He turned to me.

"Kestrella. Do you want to deactivate your tag too and leave a copy here, and then Dominic wouldn't have to come with you?"

The thought hadn't occurred to me. "N-no," I said. "I don't think I dare."

"OK." He shrugged, turning to Mark. "What are we waiting for? Let's go."

Dominic, Mark, Johnny and I walked out of the apartment leaving the gadget, Johnny's alter ego, beeping away behind us. I ran ahead of Johnny down some steps to where Mark's car, a hydrogen fuel cell Rapide Mark II, was waiting. The wail of a Gene Police van nearby made us all start. I turned round to see Johnny putting his hood up, his camera scanning all around anxiously. He wasn't looking where he was going. I saw he was about to trip over a low railing and ran back.

"Johnny!" I cried.

Too late – he fell forward, but luckily I was near enough to catch him. My arms went around him and supported him, while his went around me, with his full weight against my body. He instinctively started to pull back, but I was reluctant to let go.

"Are you all right?" I breathed.

He stayed in my arms long enough for me to feel his heartbeat slow and his muscles relax as the Gene Police van's wail faded away — it must have been after some other poor hybrid. I felt his ribs beneath his clothing, felt his long fingers on my shoulders as my own heartbeat increased.

"Hey, you two! Come on!" shouted Mark.

"Thanks," Johnny said, all low, to me. We pulled away from each other, a bit embarrassed, and hurried to the car.

Dominic and Mark sat in the front, with Johnny and I in the back. Johnny's hoodie well over his head, we cruised out of London on a virtually deserted Essex Road.

"I thought we'd just go on a recce this time," said Mark as he steered his way through the light traffic. "You know, check out the lie of the land. Then we can come back and formulate a plan of action. So I haven't told Cheri. No point. She's one busy lady."

"No, no need to bother her," agreed Johnny.

I felt a little uncomfortable about the fact that Cheri didn't know what we were doing. But it would probably be all right. After all, what could go wrong? I couldn't think straight. I was very aware of how Johnny's and my legs were touching. My fingers were groping towards his hand.

"There's maps in the back if you want to study them," said Mark.

Johnny's hand quickly picked up a map and he started studying it. I put my own hand back in my lap.

"Actually, I've been doing a little research," announced Johnny. "There's a peace camp next to the Centre. Dunno what it's like. Or why they're there. They've got a website and they say visitors are welcome. They might be able to tell us a thing or two, mightn't they?"

Mark shrugged. "Sure, why not? Although in my experience just because someone is bearing witness, it doesn't necessarily mean they are reliable witnesses."

"But any information must be worth something," I said. "I think that's a really good idea, Johnny."

For ages we never left the urban sprawl. Every mile or so we'd pass an exchange, full of jostling crowds pouring in and out carrying all manner of stuff. A lot of people thought that you were more likely to catch the disease if you spent a long time close to the same piece of technology. So these markets had sprung up full of people swapping their microwave/car/hi-fi/razor/PDA/whatever for different models.

"I've got a friend who spends half his time wheeling and dealing in these places," said Mark. "He's made a fortune. Of course, there is no statistical proof that people who continually swap their goods are less likely to catch Creep. But that doesn't stop them."

"Superstition," said Johnny. "That's what it is. They believe anything."

"Small wonder," observed Mark. "When you think what science has given us. People like you!"

"I hope that was a joke, Mark," said Johnny.

Now we were out of the city, but this wasn't countryside. Rows of heated greenhouses and battery farms of hens and pigs were occasionally interrupted by refineries and power stations burning rubbish and anything else they could get their hands on for electricity. Mark pointed out the chemical works where milk was produced directly from grass using genetically-engineered bacteria, or where meat of an unspecified nature was produced in a similar way. "They say it's just for pet food…"

The buildings glowed with ultraviolet light. "See?" Mark continued, almost gleefully. "The countryside is doing its traditional job of producing eggs, meat and milk for the population." He pointed out the fields, radiant for miles with GM rape and hemp for making cooking oil for powering vehicles. "Their fibres make clothes and fabrics."

Every now and then we saw a few trees but no birds. Not, that is, until we came to an area near the flooded mouth of the Thames, windswept and bleak beneath the steel sky, where scavenging gulls and kites circled over the old landfill sites now too polluted to be used for settlements or factories.

"I've never seen any of this place before," I said.

"Why would anyone come here who didn't have to?" continued Mark. "They tried once to use bacteria to clean up the pollution, but the bacteria mutated and just produced other toxins. They tried to house people – see those ruins? But no one could put up with the smell. That's why they built the Centre for Genetic Rehabilitation out here."

We stopped the car. Five hundred metres away across the flat, stinking marshland was a cluster of buildings surrounded by a steel wall topped with barbed wire.

A feeder road led from the main road. "Here we are," Mark said, stabbing a finger at a point on the map Johnny was still holding. "Notice anything?"

"There's no buildings marked on the map here," said Johnny.

"Exactly. This place doesn't exist on any map, just like a lot of military installations. Except it's not supposed to be a military base. It's supposed to be a research hospital to care for people like you."

Slate grey as the sky it was, a sprawl of prefabricated units with few windows and no identifying features. Mark took out his camera and began filming. As he was doing so a Gene Police van trundled along the road from London and turned down the access road to the Centre. It drove towards the checkpoint at the entrance to the complex, passing a cluster of tents and caravans that I hadn't noticed before because they were in a slight dip. From one of them a rainbow flag fluttered rather forlornly.

"What's that?" I said.

"Must be the peace camp," said Johnny. "Let's go and say hello."

Whatever they might be able to tell us, I didn't think it would be how to get in. The complex looked totally impregnable.

11. Captured

Mark, Kestrella and I were sitting around in a circle inside a Grand Lodge, which was the peace campers' fancy name for a big round tipi.

Dominic sat behind his shades outside the circle, impassive and silent as always. He hardly ever seemed to say anything, never moving unless he had to, and even then with a self-contained economy of effort. I was beginning to wonder about him – what was he thinking as he followed Kestrella like a shadow?

A small fire crackled in the centre and smoke drifted up to disappear through a smoke hole. About twenty people including ourselves were in the circle, and coffee and home-made soup had been passed around, followed by joint after joint which we three all passed up. How was I going to smoke anyway? What a joke. Now I was being talked at by this relic who looked like a throwback to the 1990s and called himself Sunfire.

"So, er, how do you get high if you can't smoke or take pills?" he drawled, eyes flicking in and out of focus. He was dressed in a scruffy old poncho.

"I don't want to get high," I said, wondering how I was going to get any sensible information out of him.

"Why not? This stuff gets too much, don't you think? You need to chill out once in a while."

"You don't understand. I'm fighting to hold on every moment of my life. Reality is all I've got. If I lose it, chances are I'll never get it back."

I could see Kestrella and Mark grilling a self-proclaimed Buddhist on the opposite side of the circle. Mark was filming him at the same time. I was not going to get any help from them.

"Too bad." Sunfire took another long toke on his joint and swayed. He obviously hadn't a clue what I was on about. I surged with contempt for these sad people. They told us they'd been camping here for six months and "bearing witness" to what they called the "unspeakable horrors" within the Centre. I did a quick area scan and realised that there was electronic sensing equipment around. We were probably being monitored.

"They do experiments. It's all run by the pharmacos," a girl called Treebabe had told us. "The drug companies."

Mark asked if we could see any evidence of medical companies' presence there.

"We don't exactly have any direct evidence," Sunfire said. "But we've been filming every vehicle that comes and goes."

Mark perked up. "Really? May I see some of the footage?"

A bloke called Geoff played some of it back on a solar-powered monitor. It had been recorded on a phone – nowhere near broadcast quality. Mark was disappointed. It didn't show anything but vans – Gene Police and unmarked cars and service vehicles.

I showed them my pictures of Jacquelyn. "Ever seen this woman being taken inside?" I asked.

They shook their heads. "You can never see who's inside the vans. They don't have windows," said Treebabe. "But there's loads of service vehicles every day so there must be a sizeable community inside."

"Do you get any hassle?" asked Mark.

"They generally started to leave us alone once they realised none of us were hybrids, you know?" said Treebabe.

"Do you get support from the locals?" asked Mark. "I mean, do they approve of what you're doing?"

"Nah, they don't trust us. I guess it's because they work in the Centre and depend on it for their livelihood, yeah?"

"Yeah, they've been bought off, man," said Sunfire.

"And have you ever been inside? Can you break in? Scale the fence?" I asked.

"No way. It's alarmed, electrified and fortified."

"There must be a weak point somewhere?"

"The far side of the wall ends at the river and the mudbanks. You can't get round there. Before that there is a small wood – well, a bit of wasteland with a jungle of brambles. They've really picked the site well."

"Have you not had the idea," asked Mark, "of a mass break-in as a protest? If enough of you just tried to scale the wall, perhaps at night time, you could get in?"

They looked at each other silently. The Buddhist put his fingers to his lips and pointed outside, then nodded in affirmation. But out loud he said, "There aren't enough of us for that. We're content just to stay here." I wondered what was really going on.

"Change as big as what we want won't happen overnight," said Sunfire, taking another toke. "Besides, we believe in non-violence, y'know? Simply by being here, we are their conscience and the embodiment of the eternal earth spirit. We will wear them down as water wears stone, slowly but surely."

Suddenly the roar of huge vehicles screaming to a halt outside the tent caused us to jump. Their headlights shone brightly through the thick canvas of the tipi. Everyone stood up.

"It's a raid!"

"Hide the stash!"

But somehow I didn't think whoever was out there was interested in the drugs. Huge shadows moved over the tipi's skin, projected by the headlights and shrinking as they approached the entrance flap. Dominic sprang into action. He leapt forward and grabbed both my arm and Kestrella's and ushered us towards the opposite side of the tent, hissing, "Quick, underneath the canvas."

He pushed Kestrella first, of course. She slid on the grass beneath the canvas and I followed with difficulty. Dominic rolled under after me just as the first of the Gene Police officers pushed their way into the tipi. He saw us escaping and shouted.

Dominic pointed to a cluster of gorse bushes in front of some young birch trees. "Quick, over there! They'll be round here in no time."

Kestrella ran ahead — she was fast. Me, I don't do much running. I always was a bit physically awkward and I struggled to keep a few metres behind them. They disappeared into the thicket as I tripped over a tussock of grass and tumbled to the ground. I had just enough time to put my hands out to break my fall, otherwise I might have broken my screen, something I'm always having nightmares about doing.

I looked back and saw two figures running up in the familiar white sealed overalls and gas masks, the insignia of the Gene Police on their arms and backs. Although probably practical, their appearance instilled fear. In all my time on the run, I'd never been so close to the Gene Police. I'd been lucky. I'd always managed to be somewhere else or merge into the shadows or a crowd, keeping one step ahead.

Before I could clamber to my feet they grabbed my legs. I didn't struggle but made my body as limp and heavy as possible. I cursed myself. It was almost as if we'd walked into an open trap.

They gripped me roughly and pushed me down. Through his plastic visor, I recognised one of them: Malcolm Winter, the Gene Police's operational commander. He spoke into a microphone inside his headpiece, his voice metallic and muffled.

"We've apprehended one of them. The other two are still at large." He nodded to his companion. "Pursue them. Back-up's on its way."

The other man headed off towards the gorse bushes and I hoped Kestrella and Dominic had had enough of a head start.

Winter's voice hissed metallically through the filter. "Game over, lad. Come on, let's see what you're like." I found myself cowering low, trying to make myself invisible as his gloved hand reached out for my hood. I wanted to fight him away, but I knew it would only make things worse. I felt overcome by shame as he threw the hood back from my head and exposed my screen. I kept facing the ground so he wouldn't see it properly. I wanted to shrink, become smaller and smaller, until I was one of those particles of soil in front of me. He grabbed hold of the shoulder of my hoodie and jerked me upwards but still I refused to face him.

"Now now, don't be shy," I heard him say. "I've seen worse, you know."

He thought I was embarrassed because I was ugly or disfigured. Instead, I'm embarrassed because people think I'm a monster. But I'm not a monster, I'm just ill. And I can do things most people can only dream of. I shook his hand off and turned to face him at last with a snake on my screen hissing at him. If he was going to hiss at me, I might as well hiss back, I thought.

"Whoa. A real snake in the grass eh? All right. Off we go, laddie." He pulled me to my feet and pushed me ahead, towards where their vans were parked by the tents.

I think the thing about the Gene Police I hate most is their sense of humour, as if it's all a big game, like paintball, and if you don't laugh it's because you're not being sporty enough. It's a tactic bullies used when I was at school. The response which I perfected was to offer no reaction, since any response – fear or resistance – is like throwing petrol on a fire. So I made my screen go dead and kept silent.

Winter pushed me up into a van. I saw Mark being bundled into another van and one of the officers carrying his camera. Inside, mine was kitted out as a mobile interview room. Winter made me sit behind a tiny desk and went back out without saying a word.

By turning up the sensitivity of my microphone I could hear what was going on outside. The major was having a difference of opinion with his two seconds-in-command, whom we had passed on the way to the van: a tall thin one who, I read on his badge, was a Lieutenant Calme, and a short round one named Dr Welcombe. I thought they looked like Laurel and Hardy.

Calme – he had a squeaky voice – was saying I had to be analysed. "That one, the computer boy. He's interesting. Unusual."

"As the medical advisor I ought to inspect him." The doctor's voice sounded sinister.

"Your request is noted, doctor. Perhaps later," said Winter. "Any news on the other two?"

"Not yet, sir." Good. Perhaps Kestrella and Dominic had managed to get away.

"With respect, sir," oozed the lieutenant, "shouldn't our happy campers be charged with harbouring a Grey?"

"Yes, that's worth six months," put in Welcombe. "It's about time we cleared this lot off."

"I disagree," said Winter. "They're useful where they are. Besides, he's not a Grey – he has a tag. Lieutenant, go and deal with the journalist. Welcombe, alert the Centre to prepare for a visitor."

Suddenly, the major was in the van, in a gust of cold air. He seated himself opposite me and I was able to get a clear view of his face through his visor. He had a long thick nose and a small moustache. His blue eyes narrowed at me as he hit some keys on a keyboard. He watched the screen, which I couldn't see. When he spoke, it was with calm, measured tones.

"If you co-operate it will be much easier for you. Let's begin with your name?"

I stayed silent and thought about Bruce Lee. When I was younger I watched his movies over and over again – and *The Bruce Lee Story*. I devoured whatever I could find about him. He was my hero, not because of his incredible fighting ability but because of his self-control. He worked out his own system of kung fu by studying all the different styles and forms of meditation and eastern philosophy. For him, it was all about self-development and learning to be aware of your environment and how to deal with it most effectively. So what would he do in this situation?

"If you won't co-operate I'll send in Dr Welcombe. He's looking forward to examining you. Well, lad?"

Come on, Bruce, give me an answer. Suddenly it came to me. Why not ask them exactly what I wanted to know? To do this, I'd have to give them something first that must be true, and it might as well be my name. So Major Winter typed Johnny Online into his database. He raised an eyebrow as a record came up.

"Have you deactivated your tag somehow? According

to this you're somewhere else completely right now. I wonder how you managed that? Bit of a boffin, are you? It wouldn't surprise me; you're obviously packing a substantial bit of processing power." He noticed something else on the computer. "I must say that I'm disappointed with your carer. She's not here, is she? She should know better, a woman in her position. This won't go down well on her record, you know."

I winced. I'd made another stupid mistake. I'd forgotten about that completely. I hoped I hadn't got Cheri into too much trouble.

"Cheri doesn't know anything about it," I said. "I did it without her knowledge."

"That probably wasn't difficult. She's a very busy woman. You do know we're related, don't you?"

Sometimes it's an advantage not having a face. It doesn't give away what you're feeling — otherwise he would have seen my jaw drop on to his desk.

"She's my cousin. Didn't she tell you? She's quite proud of the fact that we represent opposite sides of the war on Creep."

"You must detest her then," I said.

"Not at all. I admire her compassion; we need people like her."

"Huh?"

But he fell silent on the subject and I assumed he was being ironic in the way grown-ups are sometimes, part of this game he saw himself playing. "What are you doing here?" he asked.

I might as well tell the truth, I thought. "We're looking for someone. She's gone missing. We thought she might be in the CGR."

"Are you now? And who might she be?"

"Jacquelyn Chu."

"My other cousin? Missing?" Winter leant forwards.

"You didn't know? Her husband said he'd reported it. He said he'd asked your lot if they knew anything. So did Cheri."

Winter considered this. "If it's true, I can find out." He began to interrogate his computer.

While this was going on I'd been monitoring what was going on outside. Calme hadn't been long with Mark. I got the impression they'd confiscated his camera. They were now griping about Winter; I caught phrases such as "The Major is such a wimp" and "People like that should be made an example of".

I also sensed the presence of a wireless network and began tentatively to explore the on-vehicle system – it was wide open. It was easy to probe inside. Here were minutes, reports, databases. My record right up front.

There seemed to be loads about me. I had time to see 'Potential terrorist'. Me? A terrorist? But that wasn't what I was looking for. Conveniently, there was a database called 'Missing Persons'. Winter must be in there right now. I searched it – and there it was – Chu, J. reported missing fourteen days ago. Right next to the entry was the note, in red capital letters: CLASSIFIED INFORMATION. But Winter had finished looking at the file and closed it. He was examining me, the tips of his fingers together. I left that network and returned my attention to the room, noticing how the skin around his nails was frayed but his nails were carefully manicured.

"We have no record of her being reported missing," I heard him say. "Is she really?"

For a moment I was completely stunned, but again I kept my screen blank. His gaze was steady and he didn't look as if he was lying at all. And yet I couldn't let him know what I'd seen or I'd be in even deeper trouble and not able to access his network again if I ever needed to. "Of course she's missing. Her daughter and her dad are frantic." I didn't want to say that Kestrella had been with me, otherwise they'd track her tag and be on to her in no time. I hoped Mark had the sense to do the same.

"I see," he said. "Well, I'll make a note of it and tell everyone to be alert. We'll get in touch with her husband

and get all the details off him. I don't think it's any of your concern now. I just have to take a few more details and then we'll pop you next door."

"Next door?"

"Yes, of course. The Centre for Genetic Rehabilitation."

I felt panic welling up inside. He was making it sound as if we would be going to the neighbour's for a cup of tea. "But you can't – you can't take me in there. I'm a Blue."

The major sighed. "Being out without your carer is breaking a condition of your licence. The law says it's therefore void. You're reclassified as a Red. We'll inform Cheri."

"But—"

"No doubt you've heard many terrible stories about what goes on in the Centre. They're all rumours. I can assure you, having visited the place many times, that you'll be cared for. I imagine your recent life has not been particularly pleasant or comfortable. You will be comfortable there and in good hands. Now, shall I put down Cheri's address?"

I passed the next few minutes in a daze and don't recall what I said. Soon I was being hustled into the back of another van and driven towards the gates of the Centre. Dr Welcombe sat alongside me, examining me closely, looking at my transition points, photographing everything with a small PDA. He asked me about my condition. I answered irritably.

"Isn't it obvious?"

"Does it function?" he asked.

"'Course it does," I said. The whole time I had been innocently running visuals from *Grand Theft Auto 97 – Bombay* on my monitor. "I play computer games on it. Would you like to play a game? I bet I can beat you at anything. Go on, name your best game."

"Er, no thank you," he said and to my relief left me alone because, due to the stress, my heart rate was rising and my points were screaming in agony. I hoped I wasn't going to faint again. I put my head between my knees, clutching it with my hands. At least I'd seen no sign of Kestrella and Dominic. I hoped they'd got away.

The back of the van was windowless, but I could sense when we pulled up at the security gate, pausing to exchange protocols. Then the van moved forwards and I heard the clang of the arm coming down decisively behind us like the gavel of a judge passing a life sentence.

I was terrified. I was now in the place I had always feared, the place where I'd heard awful operations were performed on hybrids. The place from which I had never heard of any hybrid ever coming out.

12. Mu-Tech

Dominic charged in front shoving the barbed branches of the gorse bushes aside and I stuck fast behind. The suits worn by our pursuers would protect them, but we had to ignore the painful scratches. The gorse gave way to brambles, which snatched and scratched just as much. It was all I could do to stop from crying out loud.

Soon a willow thicket took over from the brambles and the ground underfoot grew squelchy. It embraced and sucked at our feet. It was as if the whole of nature was trying to slow down our progress. Dominic indicated for us to stop for a moment. We crouched down, hidden by the thicket, and listened. Some way away we could hear dogs barking and someone crashing through the undergrowth. But the sound wasn't getting any nearer.

All the time, as my heart raced, I was thinking about Johnny. Poor Johnny! It was my fault he came here and it was my fault he'd probably be taken into the CGR and I would never see him again. It was too awful for words.

"Dominic," I whispered. "Isn't there anything we can do? Can we go and rescue him? Oh, *merde*! We have been so stupid! We had no back-up plan. We're not very good at this, are we?"

"Quiet," he whispered back. "Talk later. Pay attention to getting out of here."

Keeping an eye on the sun, we headed west and then north, hoping we'd reach the main road sooner or later. It would be suicidal to go back to Mark's car. He might be under arrest now and the Gene Police could be searching it, looking for incriminating evidence.

What would be the charge? I had no idea, I knew so little about these things. Why would they send such high-ranking officers – Malcolm Winter, no less – just to haul in a Blue who was out without his minder? Had we broken a different law? We must have done, but which one? I only knew that there had been many new laws lately. I thought that this was due to the government trying to protect the people and stop the plague spreading. But could it have something to do with what we were doing? Was it to do with Maman's disappearance? Or Mark's investigations? There were too many questions and my mind soon got tired of going round in circles.

Meanwhile, I hoped that we weren't literally going round in circles as I continued to follow Dominic, splashing on, my shoes totally waterlogged. The only sound was the shucking of feet being hauled out of the sucking swamp as he picked a path along the least boggy ground.

"What's going to happen when we reach the main road?" I asked when I thought we were far enough away to make it safe to talk.

"I'll call for another car," said Dominic, examining his mobile. He had continued to use his mobile when most people had stopped. "Huh. No signal. What about you?"

"But I think my mobile's tapped. Should I really use it?"

"Probably right," said Dominic. "Emergency legislation. Soon as they notice you using it they'll be able to pinpoint your position."

"But do you think they know it's me and you that they chased out of the tipi? Will they be looking for my signal?"

"They may have got that information out of Mark or Johnny. But you could risk it. When we get to the road, you might make a quick call to your father's mobile and tell him to send a car."

After another ten minutes we reached drier land: a field of metre-high hemp. Crouching down, we ran along the edge to within a few metres of the road. I poked my head out from the plants; over the road were a couple of silos. However, Dominic had a signal now and he called my father's phone. It was turned off.

"Oh, what are we going to do, Dominic?"

"No choice. Wait." He settled down and made himself comfortable among the plants. I imagined that he had shut his eyes behind his shades. Dominic seemed to enjoy waiting.

I made sure I couldn't be seen from the road behind a row of plants yet I could still keep an eye on the traffic. Perhaps a bus would come, or a taxi. But hardly any traffic was passing by. A faint drizzle grew into a steady downpour. My bedraggled hair dripped on to my torn coat and I felt utterly miserable.

Suddenly I saw a red Rapide pass. It looked like Mark's. It was hard to tell, but it would be a coincidence if it wasn't his. I wondered who could be driving it? If the GP were impounding it, wouldn't they be towing it? I nudged Dominic and he called Mark's number. Mark thought it essential to keep a mobile because of his job. He answered immediately.

"Dominic, where are you?" Less than a minute later, we were speeding back to London.

"They let me go," Mark grinned as he put his foot down. "More trouble than I'm worth, me. Too much bad publicity – sometimes it helps to be a documentary producer." His smile dropped. "They destroyed my footage though. And my camera. It's the new Normalisation Law they brought in last week. You're not allowed to record or document anything within a kilometre of the CGR, or any anti-epidemiological facility. A gathering of five or more people in the same area is also illegal. This must be one of the first times it's been enforced, maybe even the first."

"How do you know we're not being followed?"

"I don't," he replied. "But I think they've got enough paperwork for the time being."

"And Johnny? Did you see what happened to Johnny?" I asked, desperate for good news.

Mark's face set. "Sorry, Kestrella. They separated us straightaway to question us individually. As they escorted me away afterwards, I saw him being put into a van and driven towards the CGR. I think we've lost him." He emitted a big sigh. "We screwed up big time, didn't we?"

I felt sick inside. Oh, how must Johnny be feeling? After two years of successfully evading the Gene Police, he meets me and I lead him straight to them and into the Centre for Genetic Rehabilitation.

"Don't blame yourself, Kestrella," said Mark. "It was my idea to come here, remember? I feel like a total amateur. We'll just have to see if there's anything Cheri can do."

We went straight to Salvation House and told her. She was furious. I had never seen her this angry before. Especially that we had done this without telling her. All I could do was hang my head and keep repeating how sorry I was.

"And you – you should have known better!" She yelled at Mark. "Do you realise what this means? They could even close down Salvation House!"

"But surely not, auntie!" I cried. "Why? Over a thing like this!"

"Oh. You're too young to understand!" She said, stabbing a finger at Mark. "But he's not! He has no excuse!"

Then she shut herself in her office to phone to her cousin. We paced up and down the corridor. I was on tenterhooks. She came out fuming – clearly the news was bad.

"Malcolm seems to be enjoying this. I'm sure he thinks he's trying to teach me a lesson."

"Why? What did he say?" I asked.

"He's playing it by the book. He says I broke the law and he ought to prosecute me too. He won't let Johnny out."

"But why, auntie?"

"As his carer I should be with him at all times or keep him in my home. I certainly shouldn't let him slip his leash – lose his tag. That's worth a £10,000 fine or three months' jail. He's right."

"But you didn't know. We did it without telling you. It's our fault. If anyone should pay the fine it should be me."

"Not in the eyes of the law," put in Mark.

"I'm so sorry, Cheri," I said.

She scowled. But she was beginning to look sad rather than angry. This made me feel even more guilty. "Mark, if I didn't know better, I'd say you were using them just to get a story."

I knew her well enough to work out that this meant that was exactly what she suspected. "Do you think Winter will prosecute you?" I asked.

"No, I think he wants something from me instead, but I neither know nor care what it is right now, as long as it's not the closure of Sally House."

"Can we really not get Johnny back?"

"You don't get a second chance, honey."

"But that's not fair!"

"Neither is catching Creep," she sighed. "I've put others at risk, you see. There is a reason for the law, Kestrella. I could even lose my job."

"But no one knows how it's transmitted, right? So how do they know you've put others at risk?"

Cheri put her hands on my shoulders and gazed tiredly and with resignation into my eyes. "It's called the precautionary principle, Kestrella. When in doubt, and to be safe, you take extra care just in case. You see? I'm sorry, but Johnny's in the CGR for good now. And I'm in deep trouble."

I couldn't accept it. I hadn't just lost Maman, but the boy I'd recruited to find her, and got my aunt into trouble.

Dominic drove me home. I could only think of seeing Papa. As soon as I arrived I called for him, but he wasn't there. I phoned his office but Marion, his personal assistant, said he was locked away for a couple of days on a project and couldn't be disturbed. She would try to get a message to him.

In despair, I took a long shower and tried to let the water wash away my cares. Papa was a powerful man with lots of important friends. He could speak to someone and they could let Johnny out and he could stay here with Dominic and me. I mustn't give up hope.

I made a decision. I would go to Papa's workplace and try to talk to him. Once out of the shower I dressed in my smartest and most conservative clothes. I carefully applied my make-up and studied the effect in the mirror. Because I'd had the best of tutors – Maman – I knew that I looked impressive and at least four years older. I saluted my image, wished it the best of luck and summoned Dominic.

On the way I stopped to make a phone call at a public payphone... I'd vowed not to buy another mobile. I worried that if I used a second one my other hand would turn into a phone too and then I'd be useless. Before my first mobile had joined to me I'd used it all the time. Afterwards, even the thought of using it revolted me. Other friends of mine who were hybrids, like Julian, couldn't understand this. "It's your 'special gift'," he'd say. "Make the most of it!"

Usually, if I wanted to use a phone I used a landline or netphone. Besides, I was sure (Cheri had said) that the phone that was part of me would be tapped, that it would be used by the Gene Police, like my tag, to monitor me. But now I felt a need to speak in confidence to a friend – Julian. I told him everything that had happened.

"My mind just keeps flashing back to imagining Johnny – on his own, in a cell or something. Maybe they are operating on him, trying to find ways of cutting out his hybrid parts. You hear such awful stories, Julian!"

"That's just your mind playing tricks, Kestrella," he said. "I'm sure they're looking after him properly."

"Why am I thinking about him so much? I should be worrying about Maman! I mean I've only just met this boy."

"You couldn't be just a little bit in love with him, could you?" Julian said, in his cheeky voice. I was glad that at least he felt well enough to say such a thing.

"Don't be silly!" I said. "I hardly know him!"

"Just asking," he said. "So are you going to carry on looking for your mum?"

"How could I stop? The answer has got to be in the CGR!" I said. "Don't you think?"

"It's no good asking me, Kes…" he said, trailing off as his voice was overwhelmed by a sudden coughing fit. "It could as well be there as anywhere else."

I now felt slightly lighter as we approached the corporate HQ of Mu-Tech. But that was a mad thing he'd said about me being in love with Johnny. The sensible thing to do, part of me was telling the rest of me, was just to forget about Johnny altogether, for the likelihood was that whatever my feelings, I'd seen the last of him.

I'd only visited Papa's offices once before because he actively discouraged it. Even Maman had only been twice. A security issue, she'd said. The offices were in their own grounds and protected by a high fence, cameras and guards.

The 4x4 stopped at the security gate and I showed my ID and asked them to buzz Papa. It took ten minutes to get Marion on the line.

"I'm not going away until he comes to get me," I told her. I was infuriated that I seemed to be so down on his list of priorities. Twenty minutes later Marion came to escort Dominic and me into the marble-floored foyer of the eighteen-storey building, beneath a massive burnished steel version of the company's logo – symbolising a couple of chromosomes – up a glass lift that was so silent and fast it made my stomach drop away, and through cool, corporate corridors designed to make you feel small. Finally we came to the suite of offices that was Papa's little kingdom.

Marion ushered us in: "He's in a meeting. I'm sorry I couldn't extract him. But I think that they'll be breaking in thirty. Why don't you wait here? Would you like a drink?"

"Thanks," I said. "We'll just have water."

The water arrived shortly and then we were left alone. I sat at Papa's desk in a large leather swivel chair and turned it to face through the window on to a courtyard planted with pampas and palms. Dominic installed himself in a corner to wait – again. I got bored of the view and turned back to the room.

"Have you been here before, Dominic?" I asked.

"No."

"I bet he spends more of his time here than he does at home."

I studied on the walls stills from TV advertising campaigns, mock-ups, storyboards and, in a locked cabinet, awards from the advertising industry.

Cheekily, I then began to peek in the desk drawers, but before I'd opened all of them, my elbow touched the computer keyboard and cleared the screensaver on his monitor, revealing the inbox of his email programme. Seeing it gave me an idea. I typed Maman's email address into a search field. A list of messages promptly appeared. I sipped my water and clicked on the most recent. It was dated the day before Maman disappeared.

✉ S - you are being ridiculous. It is intolerable you should treat me this way. I'm telling you I can't stand it any more. Je m'en fou!? - Jx

I quickly read further down the earlier exchange that led to this outburst.

✉ Jacquelyn - you're putting me in a dangerous double bind. How can I be expected to choose between my work and you? Don't ask me to do that, please. - Sx

And, earlier still:

✉ ...You don't trust me. How can I live with a man who doesn't trust me? It's too much. - J

To which Papa had replied:

✉ You're being impossible. How could you expect me to reveal confidential information?

✉ It's not enough!" she replied, as if some other exchange had happened in between. "You throw me sops as if I were a pig in a pen. Give me the full meat - or I'll be forced to go elsewhere to eat.

What could this mean? I checked the sent mail folder to see the last email he'd sent her. It just read: "We'll talk when I get back." I wondered if he'd come home before she disappeared, if they'd ever had that conversation.

I slumped back in my chair feeling devastated. It had never occurred to me to question if my parents got on well. I just assumed they did, even though Papa was hardly ever home. Was this disagreement a cause of her disappearance?

The door opened and Papa strode in. He was in his shirtsleeves and his face looked lined and tired. I got up and went to him to draw attention away from the computer.

"My flower!" He greeted me with a kiss on both cheeks. "Is everything all right? Why are you here?"

I quickly told him what had happened, leaving out the bit about the peace camp for some reason I wasn't sure of – I just didn't think he'd approve of me going there. "We just went to have a look at the place. I thought – I thought Maman might be inside! We never guessed we could be arrested just for going there. There's a new law—"

"Always new laws. This is an emergency, after all. Now listen, Kestrella…" He led me to a coffee table and settled us on two of the leather armchairs around it. "I'm sure Jacquelyn is not in the CGR. I wish you'd told me before going there. I suspect that journalist of using you to get a story. I never liked him."

"No, he was being helpful. Papa, they have Johnny now. What can we do? Can you get him out?"

"Me? Why should I be able to do that?"

"Don't you know people? People who could help? People in the government?"

"Flower, it may seem to you I know a lot of important people, but I'm not really that powerful. If I ever do meet people in the government, it's usually in the Department of Trade and Industry or the Treasury, not the Home Office. And they don't talk to each other."

"Why do you think Maman is not in the CGR?"

"Because the police would have told us. Now please, Kestrella, let Dominic take you home and get a good night's sleep. It won't be long before I'm back and we can have a nice long chat, I promise. Remember, I have a private eye looking for her."

"Then why hasn't he found anything? He can't be very good, can he? And I bet he's charging you an arm and a leg!"

He sighed and stood up. "You sound just like your mother, you know, as well as looking like her."

"Well, has he found anything?"

"Quite a lot actually, but nothing firm yet. We mustn't give up hope. If she is alive, we'll find her."

"And if she isn't alive?"

He made a gesture which dismissed the idea. "And don't worry about your friend. They will look after him in the CGR – it's what it's for."

I let that pass. I'd read somewhere that if you want to get information out of people sometimes it's best to ask open-ended questions. So I said, "Is there anything else you're not telling me?"

"Like what?" he said, and the way he hesitated made me realise there was. Was it to do with the emails?

"I don't know," I said.

"Then neither do I."

"I've heard people disappear every day and are never found," I said.

"Only if they don't want to be found."

I fixed him with a direct gaze. "But she would want to be found, wouldn't she?"

He gave me a very quizzical look and then let his face break into a sad smile. "Do you think I don't lie awake at night thinking about her? She is everything to me. I couldn't believe it when she agreed to marry me. Somebody as beautiful as her. And when she stopped modelling I encouraged her to set up her charity, and made sure Mu-Tech supported it with donations." He stopped and looked lost for words. "I really must get back to my meeting. See you soon, Kestrella. And please, just stay at home and do some homework, and your piano practice. It's too dangerous to venture out. I'll be back tomorrow."

And with that he disappeared through the door he entered by. Homework. Piano practice. The very idea was absurd. I wondered how much I really knew about the father I'd always trusted.

The next day Cheri called me. "Major Winter isn't a major any more," she said.

"What do you mean?" I asked.

"I mean he's been removed from his duties," she said. "Vicky just called me. Apparently he resisted bringing in new security measures. They've put his deputy, Lieutenant Calme, in his place. A yes-man and a sadist. I'm worried. You know, they've always wanted to close Salvation House. Now they'll probably have another go."

"You mean because of Johnny?" I asked.

"Why don't you go and read a paper?" she said.

So I accessed an online news channel. It was true – the Deputy Prime Minister Hunter Cracke had replaced Winter with Lieutenant Calme. Several sites were showing a live press conference.

Behind Cracke in big letters was the government's new slogan: "Keep Britain Normal". Cracke himself was an average-sized man in a crumpled grey suit, but his head looked like it belonged to a much larger person. When he opened his mouth to speak, it was as if a dark crack in the earth was opening and the voice which came out was like a heavy object being dragged over gravel. "People of Britain," he began. "This island, which has faced invaders so many times in its history, now faces an invasion more dangerous, more insidious and more unpredictable than any in the past. But just as in the past we have stood up against the aggressors and beaten them, we will do so again."

I could hardly believe what I was hearing. He continued: "As someone has said before: 'desperate times require desperate measures'. Already thousands of our countrymen have been affected by this virus. It is infecting our DNA, the genetic substance of our identity. Unchecked it could destroy the human race, transforming it into something completely unrecognisable.

"Many of you know someone who has succumbed to this terrible disease. It may be your child, your best friend or a work colleague. But as our chief medical officer assures me, as soon as they become infected they are, genetically, no longer the person they were. No longer human. This is hard to accept, I know, but the truth. I'm not here to pretend to you that things are different from what they are. At a time like this strong leadership is required. Unless we act decisively now, we are lost. And so are all our children and grandchildren and great-grandchildren. That is the magnitude of the threat we face."

The camera closed in on his face as he delivered his conclusion. "That is why, with immediate effect, I am suspending the officer in charge of the Biological Security Force, Major Winter and replacing him with Lieutenant Calme who can provide the leadership we need. Additionally, I am placing before Parliament as a priority measure an emergency Biological Security Bill. All hybrids, whether Grey or Blue, will be housed in a single location. Anybody found illegally harbouring a hybrid will themselves be taken to this location. I ask for everybody's co-operation. I know you will all give it willingly for the sake of every healthy person in this land and for the sake of future generations.

"Thank you and goodnight."

The report showed a few journalists trying to ask a question. I caught sight of Mark Jarrett yelling something inaudible, but Cracke waved all questions aside and strode off the podium.

The broadcast finished and I stared numbly at a blank window. They were talking about me. They'd got Johnny and my mum, and now they wanted to round me up and imprison me. What was I going to do?

13. The Centre for Genetic Rehabilitation

The buildings looked harmless enough: stacks of Portakabins, where activity had overspilled from a group of prefabricated low-rise structures. They were labelled with red letters and numbers but no names, no indication of what went on inside, and their windows were either dark or covered in blinds.

Two years of successful evasion, lying low, moving from safe house to safe house, avoiding the obvious places, stealing food, sleeping rough, and then I made one mistake and the inevitable happened. I can't blame Kestrella. It was my fault.

It took three of them, led by Dr Welcombe, to march me inside. I was taken into an interview room to be processed, told to remove all my clothes, which were taken way, and given a white hospital gown.

Over the next few hours Welcombe asked me all kinds of questions and ran what he said were a few preliminary tests. I can hardly remember what I said. It all became a blur as I tried to manage my fear by drifting off into a sort of trance and thinking about Bruce Lee. I remembered a couple of things he said when teaching some students: "Your mind is the one place your opponent can't reach". And "Spread your awareness everywhere. If you focus all of it on only ten per cent of what is going on then you leave yourself vulnerable to the other ninety per cent".

So that's what I did, in order to process the whole of my new environment. To Welcombe it looked like I didn't care, with a computer game still playing on my monitor. But instead I was taking everything in, even what was behind me: the colours of the walls – magnolia; their height and width – about six by five metres; the position of the two doors; the number of light bulbs – six; the location of the power switches; the flecks of mud on Welcombe's white suit – eleven that I could see; how dirty his spectacles were behind his visor; the existence of a wireless network which I couldn't penetrate; and so on. It made me feel more secure.

Of course I was scared, but I could tell from Welcombe's eyes that he was just as scared of me, hidden behind his plastic suit, his air filter, his gloves and instruments. Welcombe was a nasty little man who seemed to enjoy noting down every particular aspect of his subjects. Perhaps he thought he was going to get a Nobel Prize one day for his research. There seemed to be no detail of my physical, biological or psychological life that he wasn't interested in – my whole medical history, how many friends I had, whether I liked hot or cold weather, my favourite food, the condition of my cardiovascular system – and the names of my parents, which I said I couldn't remember. He found this strange but didn't press the point for the moment.

Finally he got some orderlies to escort me to my cell – or private room as he called it. So far I hadn't seen any other prisoners – or patients as they called them. But in my cell I found two cots and, waiting for me, a boy my age with an MP3 player growing out of his ears.

"Yo." He grunted a greeting. "Pod's the name. Been here a week. You just come in?"

I introduced myself and dropped on the bed, exhausted, my body on fire at all my transition points. "Been here on your own all this time?" I managed to ask.

"Nah. First four days there was a kid in here with a camera growing outta his face. Gruesome. Guy was in agony and they wouldn't give him nothing. Screamed blue murder all night long. Couldn't sleep a wink. One night they came and took him away. Never seen him since."

"Seen anyone else?" I asked.

"Not much. When I'm being taken for tests or an operation. But you hear them – all along the corridors, crying or screaming or shouting. The one next door used to bang on the wall at night. They don't want us to mix."

"You mean we eat in here?"

"Uh-huh. Eat, crap – die probably."

There were a couple of CCTV cameras mounted in the corners. This was the last thing I noticed before I fell into a dreamless sleep.

In the morning an orderly brought us some disgusting brown goo which was hard for me to suck up. I soon lost count of the number of different people who took part in my processing and analysis. They injected drugs into me, gave me tests to do, I had X-rays, MRI scans, CT scans, blood samples, a painful lumbar puncture which involved sticking an enormous needle in me and which gave me a raging migraine, tissue samples and a brain scan. Dr Welcombe came in to supervise from time to time. They didn't give me any medication at this point – said they wanted to see what

I was like without it. So the soreness and pain got worse and worse. I watched Pod using his creams enviously.

I would have gone mad if I hadn't kept talking to Bruce. He said I should bide my time until I knew enough and then wait for the best moment to attack or escape. "Johnny, just remember there is a time to advance, a time to retreat and a time to wait. This is a time to wait." But it wasn't easy. My points swelled and inflammation spread out really bad on my head. If I scratched it, it bled into my hair.

Like Pod, I hardly ever saw other hybrids and when I did it was just a glimpse – a figure disappearing through a door or round a corner, their hungry rabbit eyes fixed to me for half a second. Pod and I didn't get on. I tried to talk to him, but he was so down he didn't want to do anything but play deafening music all day: bands like Toxic Gene Bomb and Smash This Machine. When I asked him to turn it down he swore at me.

"Hey. I didn't ask for you to be in here with me. Get off my back."

"But we've got to stick together," I argued. "It's us against them. Together we're stronger; we can help each other."

"Crap. Don't make no difference what we do. We're all gonna die soon anyway. At least let me go out listening to what I wanna listen to."

After two days of this I gave up, and besides, I began to run a fever. They waited two days before giving me antibiotics. Then it took a couple of days more before those kicked in. It was while I was running a temperature and hallucinating that I thought I saw a face I knew. I was aware someone had entered the room so I switched on my camera. A surgical mask and goggles were peering down at me impassively. There was something familiar about the way she was standing, the angle of her head and shoulders, and perhaps a wisp of hair sticking out from underneath her cap. But then I shut my eyes and carried on dreaming, and I was in the garden at home again, only it was full of water flowing in from all directions and I was six years old and drowning. My mum was behind the kitchen window at the sink. I could see her; she was staring at me with no expression, observing me as I struggled to get to the side as if I was an interesting specimen of insect. Eventually I made it and she returned to her washing up as if she'd just finished watching a mildly interesting incident on television.

When the fever had died down I was given a shower and a new gown. Pod had disappeared – when I asked the orderly, who by this time I had got to know was called Ahmed, he said Pod had demanded to be sent to another room because of my screaming. I hadn't realised I'd been screaming. It must have been horrible for him – drowning out his music and everything. A few hours later Ahmed unlocked my door and escorted me, still dazed, outside for the first time.

In a yard was a gathering of about two hundred hybrids. I'd never seen so many together at the same time. What a mixture: people with all sorts of boxes, bits of plastic, wires, you name it, hanging from them, poking out of them, forcing them into unnatural positions. Some were in wheelchairs, some on crutches. All bore the dead eyes and drooping shoulders of pain and misery. Remembering what had brought me here I looked around for Jacquelyn, but failed to spot her anywhere. Everyone here was a teenager. We were surrounded by security guards, orderlies and nurses. The atmosphere was silent and expectant. Everyone was furtively peering at everyone else with a mixture of curiosity and sullen hopelessness. I searched for Pod but couldn't see him either.

On a small stage at the end stood Welcombe and Lieutenant Calme, who now seemed to be a major judging by the stripes on his suit.

"OK, shut up, everyone," yelled Calme, although no one was talking. "The only reason why you're all here today is because we have a visitor who wants to see you.

It won't take long. You are not permitted to talk to each other during this time. If asked, you will tell him how well you're being cared for. Afterwards, you will return to your rooms immediately."

He then turned to mutter something to Welcombe. A door into one of the admin buildings opened to admit a medium-height woman of about fifty, who strode to the stage. For the first time since entering the CGR I was seeing a healthy human who wasn't wearing any kind of protective clothing. Her straight grey hair was in a no-nonsense cut and beneath her white coat she wore practical clothes. The result was that she was almost unnoticeable; even her body language made its best attempt to deny her presence. But of course, with a lurch in my stomach, I recognised her at once.

My mum had always looked like that from the first time I could remember, as if she was always trying to deny herself any expression of style or personality. I tried to hide behind someone, but she didn't look in my direction. Instead, she was preoccupied with the person accompanying her – Hunter Cracke, the Deputy Prime Minister, just recognisable through his visor. She was chatting, indicating some of the inmates, gesturing around as if explaining what went on here, and he nodded and occasionally asked questions. He seemed very nervous.

Upon reaching Calme and Welcombe, they shook hands and shared a private joke, which they laughed at but neither he nor my mum did. Cracke stood there for a while, surveying us as they talked to him. He pointed at a few of us, who shifted uncomfortably. He appeared to be asking questions. Abruptly, without addressing us with a single word, he turned to my mum and she escorted him away, followed briskly by Calme and Welcombe. Slowly, we were moved off, gazing at each other with unspoken yearning for contact.

Was that it? What the hell was my mother doing here? How come she knew the Home Secretary? Why did he want to see us?

Back in my lonely room I didn't have long to wait for some answers. Three hours later Ahmed came to take me back to the interview room. Soon she entered, sat opposite me and stared just as she had in the dream. As before, she wore no uniform, no protective clothing. I studied her face – her skin had the tired quality of a deflating balloon. She really hadn't altered much. Neither of us spoke for a while and I imagined she was examining me in the same way, observing my changes. All I was giving her was an impassive smiley face on my screen.

Finally, she spoke.

"Here we are then. You took your time. I've been waiting two years for you to turn up." Her voice was deep, vaguely impersonal and slightly cracked.

I remembered when Kestrella had asked me what I'd do if I met her again. But instead of doing what I'd said I would, I replied, "Sorry I'm late."

"No need for sarcasm. You've grown," she observed. There are no clichés like the old clichés.

"Are you the reason why I'm here?" I asked.

"Of course not, whatever gave you that idea?"

"I don't know," I said. "How do I know anything? Why am I here? What are all these tests for? What's going to happen to me?"

"All in good time," she said. "We've got plenty of time."

"I don't want time, I want my freedom."

She let a small smile irritate her thin lips. "Talking of tests, I've got your results here. They make interesting reading."

"To somebody I suppose. But why would you be interested in me after all this time?"

"I'm the chief medical officer here in case you didn't know."

I said nothing and looked away. So, I'd found my mother and my darkest fear was true – she was the enemy. When she'd found out that I had the disease, she'd thrown me out to fend for myself. Now I could see why – because I represented everything she was fighting, because she was in charge of the institution that lives in the nightmares of every Creep victim. I stood up and started to pace the room. A camera swivelled to follow me. She remained seated.

"Do you want to hear the results?" she said icily.

"What difference will it make?" I said. "It can't turn back the clock. It can't change anything."

"I don't have to tell you. But I thought you'd like to know, seeing as knowledge is power."

So far I'd forced my pixels to display only a smiley with a straight line for a mouth. Now I made the eyes narrow, the brow furrow. She gazed up at me with eyes as clear and grey as her hair. What kind of a game was she playing?

"Sit down then and I'll begin," she said.

Suddenly a memory surfaced from the childhood I'd repressed. Up until this moment, most of my childhood had been a blank. But now I recalled my mum and me at about six years old; it was bedtime and she held a picture book; I was racing around my bedroom and she wanted me to go to bed. She was waiting to read me a story and I was ignoring her, but she was saying, "Come and sit down beside me and I'll begin." I realised I'd been clenching my fists so hard my nails were hurting my palms. I unclenched them and returned to my chair.

"Thank you," she said and opened the folder on the desk in front of her. "You might like to know that you have raised quite a few eyebrows here. It's not often we get a case like yours. In fact, I should say it is quite unique."

"Bully for you," I grunted.

"Yes. Quite. Medically, you are not in good condition, but that's not surprising if you've spent two years on the streets. Indeed, I'm quite impressed. And your friends at Salvation House have looked after you recently."

"They're not my friends," I said.

"Whatever," she said dismissively and began to study her files. "Anyway, as you may or may not know, most hybridisations are site-specific. There is a definite interface between the organic, human body and the inorganic, electrically-powered element. But although you have two such sites at the front of your head and on your arm, there's also circuitry spread throughout your body.

"Quantum-level nanotech microprocessors communicate using the tiny electric field that occurs naturally on the surface of your skin. Data is transmitted by modulating the field minutely in a similar manner to how a radio carrier wave is modulated. Implanted around your body are the bits of hardware which your computer uses, such as the modem, hard drive and processor. Naturally, most of the components are nanotech. So the inorganic-organic interfaces are engineered proteins similar to computer chips, connected to the same molecule-thin filaments that are used by all nanotech electronics. Are you following me?"

"Uh-huh," I said in a sort of noncommittal way.

"And these interfaces are all over your body. Because they are nanotech and made out of protein, written by RNA, they reproduce, and therefore we can analyse the DNA. But as far as you are concerned it means that the situation is not static, as it were."

Now I was worried. "What do you mean?"

"I mean it's developing. In layman's terms, you are gradually turning more and more into a giant biological computer."

I turned my camera on to my hands and stared at them. They looked just the same as they always had. Skin, nails, fingers.

"It's giving us some insight anyway into the changing nature of the virus. That's not static either, you know. If it was, we might have nailed it already."

"You mean you're using me… to find a cure?" I said.

"Oh, come on. We use everybody here. What do you think this place is for? How can we do anything else – animals don't get the plague. They don't use technology. We have to study humans."

"Whether they like it or not," I said.

For the first time her eyes betrayed a flash of emotion. "There's a war going on, Robert, a biological war. In wartime you have to compromise; you have to make sacrifices for the greater good. The sooner you understand this the better."

She'd called me Robert. I'd forgotten. That was my real name. How long had it been since somebody had called me that?

"My name isn't Robert," I said. "Haven't you got it written down there? I'm Johnny."

"Well, here we go by what is on your birth certificate. And I suppose I should know what that is."

"So. I'm the sacrifice, am I?"

"You're not the only one," she said, pursing her lips. "The greater good. You have to think of the greater good."

"What is the greater good?" I said angrily. "Something bigger than me that I don't feel part of. Is one group of people allowed to exploit another just because there are more of them, in the name of the greater good?"

For the first time, a small little crackle of a laugh escaped her, devoid of humour. "My, you've become quite the philosopher, haven't you? Yes, I've read your little blog site, with its immature adolescent rants. I tried to use it to find you, but you're too smart for that – you deserve some credit. Well, no doubt one can come up with a philosophy which justifies almost any behaviour. But this is our policy and it's one I happen to agree with, which is why I have this job and why the political party which appointed me has so much support among the public." She stood up, gathering her files together. "Consultation over. I have another appointment. Unless—"

I stood up. "I have another question," I said.

She looked at me and for the first time I sensed an element of anxiety. My mind was fit to explode with questions, but perhaps some of them I didn't really want to know the answer to. Not yet anyway. Almost inadvertently, my brain decided to ask one of the most innocuous.

"Can I make a phone call?"

14. Hidden Letters

For the first time in my recent life I couldn't be bothered to put my make-up on in the morning. I stared at Dominic across the breakfast table, wild-eyed and confused, but I couldn't talk to him – he was paid to be my minder, not my mentor. He just waited and looked at the world through his tinted spectacles as if they could filter out all the things he didn't like. I felt a wave of disgust. How could he know what it was like to be me? Did he feel contempt, pity – or indifference? Was I a spoilt rich kid getting what was coming to her?

Did he think I deserved what I got as he saw my life disintegrating around me?

I felt myself starting to cry, but didn't want him to see, so I rushed into the bathroom. I mechanically applied cream to my transition point, not that it seemed to make much difference these days. Perhaps I was becoming immune to it.

When I'd calmed down, I left the bathroom and went straight into Papa's part of the apartment. I wasn't supposed to go in here and it was kept locked, but I knew where the spare key was hidden.

I didn't know what I was looking for, but in a kind of blind panic I was in his drawers, his wardrobe, his bureau, under his bed, looking under piles of clothes and papers, or behind the bookshelves. After a while, I gave up and flopped back on his bed to stare at the ceiling, breathing heavily. I was being stupid or paranoid. Maman and Papa had just been having a normal marital squabble, that's all. I shouldn't be reading anything into it, and the only reason I was was because Maman had disappeared. It was mad to think that Papa would have murdered Maman and hidden the body somewhere.

I gazed around the bedroom – its walls covered with Edo tapestries showing peacocks and courtesans – then walked into his den, the outer room. Here were his toys, which he hardly ever had time to use nowadays – his telescope, his media centre, his collection of old manga and anime. The display cabinet holding a collection of samurai swords and Japanese robes. The curved swords with their delicate inlays around the handguards and on the scabbards. I had always taken these things for granted, but now I realised how much they meant to him. They were mementoes, like an umbilical cord stretching halfway round the world, connecting him to his ancestors and his culture. After all, whenever anybody looked at Papa they saw Japan. It was written in his face and in his genes. It was the same for me too. I was half French and half Japanese, but here I was in a third country, Britain, unable to leave, and with my genes irrevocably altered as a result. Any chance of a normal life had been destroyed.

And the government had the gall to go on about Keep Britain Normal.

Was I British? Would I have been normal even before I caught Creep? At that moment I hated Britain and its pompous self-righteousness. Another wave of revulsion overcame me. I went over to the cabinet and stared at a Noh robe from the 18th century. The embroidery was so exquisite – bamboo and birds.

Impulsively, I opened the cabinet and took it out. The material was heavy – silk embroidery and gold leaf on satin lined with fine satin quilt. It had so many strange folds – I couldn't resist slipping my arms into the sleeves. It was slightly too big, but the padded shoulders disguised this. I sashayed back into the bedroom to examine myself in the mirror on the wardrobe door. I twirled around and admired how exotic and really Japanese I suddenly looked, thrusting my hand and phone into each of the large pockets to prevent the robe swinging out too much. Then, in the right pocket, I sensed something – something that felt like a large envelope. Reaching awkwardly round with my right hand I pulled out a manila envelope bearing Papa's name and address written in Maman's handwriting. My heart stopped and I sat down on the bed suddenly.

"Kestrella! Where are you?" A voice startled me. It was Dominic's. I had said we would go out to Sally House after breakfast.

I tried to level my own voice and shouted, "I'm in here. I won't be long."

My hand shaking, for no good reason, I opened the envelope. Inside was a bunch of smaller envelopes – all addressed to me, all in Maman's handwriting. And they had all been opened. I couldn't believe it. Quickly I read the first one, scribbled on a piece of lined notepaper.

> *My darling,*
>
> *I know you'll be upset at my sudden disappearance, but please don't worry. I'm quite all right. I had to do it and when I explain I hope you can understand why I couldn't say goodbye.*
>
> *Recently I met somebody, a young man, who told me something which at first I didn't believe.*

But then he showed me some evidence and gradually I came to see that it must be true. Kestrella, I don't want you to be upset, but I know you're worried about having caught Creep, and more than anything else you and I want a cure. But one thing I can promise you – you won't get it from your father's company or from the government, no matter what they say. Exactly why this is I can't say now. Your reaction will probably be like mine – disbelief. Like me, you'll need to see the evidence with your own eyes first.

In my next letter I'll tell you where I am and then perhaps you can come to find me. But don't tell Papa. It wouldn't be a good idea. He'd try to stop you or, worse still, come and take me away, and not just me.

Anyway, you know how much I love you. And I know you have faith in me – you know I never do anything lightly and always for the best of reasons. So trust me and remember I love you and am still here for you.

Goodbye for now,

Maman

I looked at the dates on the postmarks and opened the next letter hurriedly.

> *Dearest Kes,*
>
> *Already I miss you so much. I hope you got my last letter and are not worrying. But you must try to pretend I'm still missing otherwise they'll suspect something. I forgot to say that before and I hope everything's all right. Don't say a word to Papa.*
>
> *I said I'd tell you where I am, but I can't do that yet. We've got to move. The Gene Police found out where we are. Who are we, I hear you ask. Tell you next time. Have to help with the moving – there's lots of equipment.*
>
> *Bises,*
>
> > *Maman*

I put this away and quickly took out the third letter. This was written on the back of a piece of scrap paper.

> *Chère Kestrella, ma fille*
>
> *I miss you so much, I hope I've made the right decision because the longer I stay here the more I realise I can't come back. I've burnt my bridges.*

And I've done things I never thought I'd do before. Last night we attacked a Gene Police station with a firebomb. Can you believe this?

Merde, now I've written this I realise I can't put the address in case it falls into the wrong hands. Never mind, I'll post it anyway. Are you doing your homework? You must carry on as if life is normal. I promise we'll see each other soon.

Hugs and kisses,
ta Maman

There was a noise outside. Quickly, I stuffed the envelopes inside my T-shirt as Dominic came into the outer room. I heard him call for me. I walked to meet him, removing the robe as I went.

"I'm coming, Dominic, just looking for something. I'm going into my room to change, all right?"

I wondered why he'd followed me in here as he left the suite silently. I now began to suspect Papa might be paying him to keep an eye on me and report back. I really was getting paranoid. I replaced the robe, shut the cabinet, checked that everything in the room was as when I entered it and left, locking the door and hiding the key again.

I went into my own room and bolted the door, fished the letters out of my T-shirt and continued where I'd left off. There was one more letter.

Ma belle fille,

I must keep this brief. You must be bursting with questions. I hope you've been able to keep this from Papa. Remember, I do still love him, but I can't be with him at the moment and you'll understand why when you see me.

Have you heard of the Hybrid Resistance Army? These are the people I've joined. Please don't be shocked. They're all good people struggling for the rights of people like us. No one else's doing this. The authorities are so hard, they treat the pandemic as an enemy to be wiped out, and that means us. Look at what's happening in the name of treatment but all they want is to be cared for.

Cheri does a wonderful job, but mark my words they'll soon close down Sally House.

I think you'd better not come here however, it's too dangerous. I'll write later when I've thought of where we can meet. Until then, my love is always with you. Are you continuing to take your

medicine and put the cream on every day? It
won't be a cure, but it will make you feel better. I
wish I was there to do it for you.

Bises, Maman.

I put the letters away in a safe place – a locked box where I kept other important stuff like my diary, letters from friends, a ring a boy in year nine once gave to me, a photograph of another boy at school I had a crush on until he found out I was a hybrid and then wouldn't talk to me any more. I put the key on a chain round my neck, quickly slipped on a T-shirt with a cartoon character on it to make believe I felt carefree, and gazed as if for the last time around my bedroom. Everything about it seemed suddenly precious. I feasted my eyes on the manga posters, my games and books, my little Zen garden with its bonsai cedar and miniature shrine that I'd nurtured since I was eight. My other childhood relics – soft toy anime characters, French dolls, old clothes, photos of Maman on old magazine covers. I knew I was seeing them for the last time. The authorities would come and get me and take me to this place they were getting ready. I didn't want to leave. I was happy here. I fought back tears and left the room, locking it.

"Dominic!" I called as singsong as I could manage. "Aren't you ready yet because I am!"

As we went down in the lift I found myself humming a song. Maman was alive! And suddenly I began to think about the Hybrid Resistance Army, bombs and ways to get Johnny out of the Centre for Genetic Rehabilitation…

At Salvation House, the atmosphere was completely different from before. It was packed with people coming from outside, smelling of rain and sweat and uncertainty. A dozen conversations were going on at once and I pushed my way through hybrids, carers, supporters and helpers to get to Cheri's office.

Somebody I recognised but didn't know was in the middle of talking: "This is the moment we've always feared. When they'd come for us with all the power of the state and take us away instead of letting us take care of each other. Up to now they've been treating us with kid gloves, but now the gloves are off."

"You're right," Cheri replied. "I thought this might happen. But it's almost as if there's been a power coup in the centre of government."

"Yes, where's the Prime Minister? He's the one we elected, not this fascist block of stone!" asked somebody else, and then the room split into three different conversations.

Mark appeared, breathless. "I was at the press conference," he announced. "Cracke's spin doctor almost had the police throw us out as soon as anybody tried to ask an interesting question."

"What about us?" I asked. "What's going to happen to us?"

"I think they're going to designate an estate in South London that was earmarked for demolition as a place to take all hybrids. It's going to be a kind of mass quarantine camp, to prevent you infecting everybody else."

"But that's ridiculous!" said five people at once, including me. And then I continued: "Nobody knows what causes Creep – and if people could catch it just from being next to somebody with the disease then everybody would have it by now, especially somebody like Cheri! She works with hybrids all the time!"

"It's not rational, I know," said Mark. "It's superstition. Like during the Black Death people would sacrifice animals, but of course that didn't stop the plague either. It's fear, pure and simple. They don't know what to do and they've got to appear as if they do to impress the healthy electorate."

One of Cheri's fellow workers burst out: "Now they're going to close the hospice where will we put everybody?"

Another said: "More to the point, do we co-operate?"

"We can't – how can we care for people when they're in a ghetto?"

"We have to organise a mass resistance!"

"If they're going to get heavy, we have to respond in kind!"

"I'd rather see what we can negotiate first," said Cheri.

"Oh, Cheri," said another, "they don't want to negotiate! It's got beyond that."

I left them to their political discussions. It was all right for them – they were normal. At the end of the day they could always go back to their normal houses, apartments, families. They all knew each other. For them this was just another political game, however well-meaning they were. They could never know what it was like. Not until they caught Creep themselves, and then there would be no going back.

Outside I met a girl I knew – a Blue called Carrie – with her mum. She also had a mobile phone, but was left-handed. She looked desperate.

"We're going to have to escape," she said. "There must be lots like us all thinking the same thing right now. They'll be on the net plotting where they're gonna meet."

"But the police'll be monitoring those sites."

"Yeah, you're right. For all we know they're monitoring us right now. We've got to act immediately. It'll be a week or so before they set the checkpoints up. We've got time to find somewhere to hide," she said.

"It's OK for me and you: with our hands in our pockets we can pass for normal. But some of us…" I was thinking of Johnny "…how can they go anywhere without being spotted?"

I left her and made my way along the busy corridor to find Julian's room. Inside it was quieter; the smell of bitter almonds was even more intense, but mixed with a kind of sickly sweetness. Julian was dozing but opened his eyes when he heard me enter. He'd lost weight again and his skin was blotchy.

When he spoke his voice was like sandpaper.

"Kestrella! Come sit down here." He gestured to the chair by his bed. "Give me a kiss, that's it!"

I did so. "Julian. How are you?"

"Oh, better than I look probably. It's these damn drugs they've been giving me. But Angie says I should be up and around soon." He struggled to sit up but lapsed back. "Can you be an angel and pass that water? I've been thinking about you," he said as he sipped. "Has your mother turned up?"

"Yes, she has! Or at least I've found some letters which prove she's alive – letters my father's been keeping from me!" And I told him the story. His eyes as he listened became even more blue and intense within their dark wells.

"Julian – have you heard of the Hybrid Resistance Army?"

"Oh, aye – it's basically a nutter who calls himself Thom Gunn. He was one of the first hybrids who managed to stay Grey. He tried to recruit me once when I was a bit more active, and I told him where he could get off. He's a shooting fanatic – you know what his condition is?"

I shook my head.

"He spent so much time in the shooting range that his arm turned into a rifle." I remembered the man who'd fought off the attack on Sally House a fortnight ago. "You're not thinking of joining them?" he asked.

"Oh no – certainly not."

"Please don't – violence never gets you anywhere, it just puts you in the line of fire."

"But my maman – she says she's joined. I have to find her. Where do you think I should start looking?"

"That's tough. If they were easy to find, the Gene Police would have caught them. But if I was going to start looking, I know where I'd go." He broke off to succumb to an extended coughing fit.

"Where's that, Julian? Please tell me." I handed him a bowl to spit into. There was blood in it.

"The last I heard they were in Deptford, South London. That's where I'd go." He started coughing again. "Arcade just off the New Kent Road called The Soft Machine."

"Thanks, Julian. I won't make you talk any more – you just concentrate on getting better."

"Wait, what about that boy – the hybrid – in the CGR?"

"Johnny? What about him?"

"Well? Should I be jealous?" he coughed.

I laughed. "Shut up! I'll pop back soon. No – quiet! *Salut!*" I kissed him on the forehead again as his lids slipped down over those deep blue eyes. Then I sneaked out to the corridor where Dominic was waiting, a corner of hope in my heart.

15. Wipe-out

All my childhood I'd lived in a house devoid of expressions of love, devoid of decoration, knick-knacks and family photos. There was nothing unnecessary and those essentials were all tidily in their place and maintained purely for function.

Afterwards, living in rundown squats where posters of rock bands and graffiti covered the damp patches and peeling plaster, I came to the conclusion that our family home was kept as if a horrible crime had been committed and somebody had gone through it with a toothcomb to remove any trace of possible evidence. In this blank space my parents came and went, observing rituals exclusively connected with work; but what this work was I was never permitted to know.

Children should be seen and not heard so I was sent to boarding school from the age of seven. For companionship I had the Internet. I watched everything from a distance. My parents lived their lives like machines – for programming read duty.

Unsurprising that I should now be turning into a machine. My featureless cell was like a home from home. In the solitude of this cell I monitored my body. My mother had told me I was becoming less and less human by the day. Yet I could still hear my heartbeat, the regular pumping of my pulses, the rasp of breath in bronchial tubes, the gurgling of my digestion, the blood pounding in my head.

But then I wasn't exactly turning into a machine but into a different kind of living organism. Was I a pioneer or the last of my kind, the end of the race? Was I alpha or omega? Was I a fruitless branch on the evolutionary tree or the budding of a strong new trunk? Quite frankly, I didn't care. I just wanted to get the hell out of there.

Naturally, they hadn't let me make that phone call.

A day passed. They put me on a new drug and immediately I had convulsions from cramps in my stomach. They said it would pass. It got worse. I screamed so loud and beat the walls so hard they gave me another drug. This made me sleepy. I don't know how long I slept. When I woke up I felt sluggish, but at least the convulsions had ended.

It goes without saying that from the moment I'd been brought to the CGR I'd been trying to detect a network to hack into. Naturally, security was tighter than a bank's and any networks were well hidden. That didn't stop me running a program which checked every five minutes to see if one had become available. It was on the third day after I saw my mum that I finally found one. Just a whisper it was, a little tendril, but I grabbed hold of it, amplified it and soon I was able to tunnel down its signal. But not very far. Instead, something was coming the other way: something big and fast, some kind of Trojan giant and before I knew what was happening it had bypassed me and my firewalls, bolting the door behind it, and spread out into my system, installing itself, making itself at home. Then the tendril withdrew and the whisper faded. I was alone with an alien invader.

I threw a container around it to isolate it. But I wasn't sure if something had already got out, some spawned child of itself budded off, disguised as another part of me, lying in wait ready to ambush some function of mine. It wasn't long before I began to feel faint. I lay down on my cot and blinked at the ceiling. A sweat broke out on my temples and I started to shake uncontrollably.

A red film spread over my 'vision' and my head start to thump. The drumming grew louder and louder and squeezing my head didn't help. It was getting hard to think. Memory blocks began to cut out. I was losing the ability to remember the names of things. I was forgetting words. I was forgetting who I was.

Numbness spread up me. I began to lose sensation of, you know, those things on the end of your legs, and the wotsits you hold stuff with. Then the stuff that comes in through flappy things you listen with faded, and the thing above my head was greying and I was wibbly-wobbly flippy-floppy. Wanted go bye-byes in the... mmmm, goo goo ga, ba, ma-ma, durrrrrrrr...

Blackness.

System shutdown.

......

_____

Hello.

Welcome to Johnny Online.

Please type in your password.

Thank you.

Where would you like to go today?

Please stand by while root-level security runs a system check, virus check, security installation...

A dangerous and unauthorised program named Creep4.exe residing in the system folder has been found and isolated, do you wish to delete it?

Deleting...

Initiating back-up restore. Please wait.

_____

I am Johnny Online, aged fifteen. I was born on a Thursday. My favourite colour is brown. I hate rice pudding and fish. Thank goodness for that. I thought I was a goner. But my immune system was clearly up to scratch. My head felt like a cylinder block, but otherwise I felt reasonable – the sluggishness and convulsions had gone. Someone came in almost immediately. I acted all sweet and innocent, said I felt fine except for a headache and asked for paracetamols. They brought them.

The team returned in their white suits with their needles to take samples, their electrodes to take readings and their clipboards to ask questions. Resistance was pointless apart from lying.

To take me to the examination room where they performed further tests Ahmed and another orderly, Joseph, would escort me along several corridors. They were completely nonchalant about my appearance – I guess they'd seen everything. Halfway there we'd pass by a series of windows through which I could see another building. About five metres cubed, this building was set apart from the others, with steel shutters on the windows and door, and encased completely in a wire mesh. The third time we passed it I asked what it was.

"That's the home of our special guest," said Ahmed.

"He is kept in isolation," said Joseph.

"Who is it then?" I asked.

"Don't know, never seen him."

"Top secret," said Joseph.

"That's right, he has his own special guard."

"Could it be a she by any chance?" I asked.

Ahmed shrugged. "Dunno. Could be, I suppose. Could be neither. You never know these days, do you?"

Each time we passed I looked at the building, small and grey, in splendid isolation. I never saw anybody come in or go out.

"Whoever or whatever is in there must be pretty dangerous," I said.

"We're just told not to have anything to do with it," said Ahmed shrugging.

"It has its own dedicated team."

The next day Ahmed and Joseph took me outside. This was new. I hadn't been outside since we'd all been to see Cracke and I wasn't exactly sure how long ago that was – my internal clock had been reset during my shutdown.

It was cloudy and the air smelt bad, with a hint of brine from the tidal Thames. I was in a paved and gravelled quad surrounded by low buildings with a few nods to the existence of nature in the form of some straggly bushes.

Joseph left Ahmed to take care of me as I felt the wind stir the hair on my head. On the far side of the square a couple of other inmates were being given a breath of fresh air – we kept casting furtive glances at each other.

Presently a door opened and my mum marched out. She dismissed Ahmed with a nod. He gave me a death look as he left and rolled his eyes towards my mother.

"Shall we walk?" she said. "I'd hate you to lose the use of your legs."

I shrugged and we started a slow circumnavigation. She studied me closely as if I was a preserved specimen and blew air heavily out through her thin lips.

"Listen, I'm very sorry about what happened. Believe me. No, I know it's hard, but it's hard for me to say it as well. They were trying out a new treatment – a combination of retrovirus and software virus to reprogramme your DNA. That means a conventional medicine and a computer program, administered simultaneously to give a two-pronged attack on the virus and its effects. It looked like it was going to work except your enhanced defence mechanism resisted it and in the end eliminated it." I didn't say anything, just carried on walking. "The boffins are back at the drawing board and no doubt they'll come up with an improved version soon."

I was about to speak but she put her hand on my arm, and it was as if I had an electric shock – this was the first time she had touched me for nearly three years.

"They're monitoring you, you know, but out here they can't tell what I'm saying – there are no cameras, unlike before in that room. You can say something innocuous if you like."

I was confused. So I said, "I'm confused."

"Naturally. The point is, they used you as a guinea pig and they want to do it again – and this time they'll hopefully have a better chance of succeeding, that is, of creating something that will reverse the effects of the RTGV. It may have some unfortunate side-effects – we're still working on trying to minimise these. So if it works, there's a possibility that it will inadvertently blank out your memory. As you found out yesterday, you would be turned into a baby all over again – mentally speaking of course. Hopefully, physically you would start to return back to normal, though our current thinking has it that some surgery would be necessary to make you look anything like normal again – in your case, considerable plastic surgery to rebuild your face, though I doubt if we'd have the budget for that."

A baby, I thought. She wants me as a baby again. But out loud I whispered through clenched teeth, "Why should you care whether I'm normal or not?"

"If you're going to take that line," her voice turned sharp, "I promise you I will leave immediately. Of course I care. I'm your mother, aren't I? Now, listen to me carefully. I'm only going to say this once." This was a tone I recognised. Impatient, obsessed with efficiency. "You will already be aware that the only way they can administer the treatment is by opening up the network to you. If you want to get out of here, exploiting that fact is your only chance."

I was stunned. Was she actually saying she was going to help me escape from the CGR, of which she was a chief honcho? Why?

"But—" I began.

"Shut up and listen. You were never very good at doing that. This is for your own good."

Not the greater good, I thought.

"When the network opens this time you will be prepared. I am going to give you a printout of the protocol and passwords. They will hopefully do it tomorrow – the schedule is for completion around 5 p.m. This will allow you not only to repulse their program and save yourself, but to access the security system which unlocks all the doors and to deactivate the CCTV cameras."

While she was saying this she was continuing to stare straight ahead and walk, as if she was discussing the weather. I kept my camera fixed on her solid, owl-like profile, hardly able to believe what I was hearing.

"How do I know I can trust you?" I said.

She looked at me as if debating how to respond. "You never know anything in this world, do you?" she said finally. "And remember to watch what you say."

Then she drew her hand from her pocket and groped for my hand. Inside her hand was a piece of crumpled up paper which I accepted. As soon as I had it she took her hand away and replaced it in her pocket. The operation was over in a second; the touch necessary was sufficient only for its purpose and nothing more. I put my hand with the paper in my pocket. We walked on a bit further.

"Of course, you may not want to do that. You may want to stay here with me and help us find a cure." Her voice was quieter now, containing a level of uncertainty which wasn't there before. "But frankly, I think you will be better waiting for the cure to be made another way."

"Thank you for giving me the choice." I nearly added 'this time'. "I'll think about it."

Suddenly she straightened herself and I realised her posture had been slumping more and more during the conversation. "I have a meeting. That's enough." She looked round for Ahmed or Joseph and nodded when she saw them behind a window. They came out and took me by the arm. My mum and I looked at each other. Her pupils were large in her grey eyes and I wondered why, and why I didn't have more to say to her, but there was a lump in my throat that I couldn't explain. "Good luck," she said.

She walked away through a door and I went off with Ahmed and Joseph.

"What a dragon, eh?" said Joseph. "Rather you than me."

"Do you know her?" I asked.

"Oh, only from a distance, I don't have any direct dealings with her."

"They call her the terrier though," said Ahmed. "On account of the fact that she snaps a lot and never lets go."

She let me go though.

They escorted me back to my cell. "Have you been

here long?" I asked them.

"Long enough, mate. About four months."

"Aren't you worried you might catch the plague?" I said.

"Nah, well, a bit, not much," replied Ahmed. "I take all the precautions. We're scanned regularly. I reckon I'm safer here than anywhere else."

"Besides," said Joseph, "if I do get ill, my contract says I'll get a pension for the rest of me life."

Ahmed turned to Joseph. "You don't believe that rubbish, do you? Did you ever hear of anybody getting it?"

When I heard the click of the key and their arguing voices receding down the corridor behind the door, it was then that I collapsed on the floor, nearly scraping my keyboard on the floor, and rolled around on my back kicking my legs in the air and hitting the wall, the floor and the bed. I don't know why. Anyone watching on the CCTV must have had all their prejudices confirmed about the weirdness of hybrids.

I had thirty hours to go. To take my mind off matters parental I memorised the passwords and protocols on the piece of paper my mother had given me and wrote them into special software that would be triggered as soon as a network connection was detected.

The next day two burly male nurses brought the drugs with my food and watched while I slurped down the noxious slurry. I sat down to wait for the network to open and the viral software to come at me. The medicine – whatever it was they had cooked up for me – made me feel drowsy again and despite my best efforts to keep awake, I lapsed into a dreamless sleep.

I woke up just in time with my brain feeling as if it carried a tonne of granite. And into this head an arrow of data suddenly shot through a blazing open window. All my nerves lit up as the data spread across my skin and into my cells like an ice cold flush, like dye on blotting paper. Then the programs I had written were initiated and a wave of my own data pulsed in the opposite direction. A semantic tussle occurred at a level almost below my awareness and at a speed beyond thought. Suddenly the incoming data was shunted aside into a specially created dump where it was isolated, and a new lump of fresh data was shot from my hard disk in the direction it had come from, radiating in the form of radio waves from the power source of my biologically generated electricity, finding a receiver and tunnelling down wires towards the server.

It was as if my way was marked by a yellow line on the floor for me to follow. Here was the security centre, part of the triple A level admin sector. Protocols and passwords accepted without quibble. A map of the establishment with circuits and security sectors. It wasn't difficult to spot my route. Here was my cell and there were the controls operating the CCTV cameras. Turn them all off – no doubt that will get people running, but hopefully in the wrong direction.

Here were the remote door locks in the event of an emergency such as a fire so that everybody could be let out. One could unlock all the doors in any section, or individual doors. I unlocked mine and was out. Into the corridor, turned right down to the end, turned left, a fire door, open, emergency exit third door on the left: open. I was in the cold dark outside. Security lights popped on. I'd forgotten about those. Looked for the control panel, but there wasn't one. Wasted precious seconds in the process, then ran alongside the building hoping no one could see me. Well, it was dusk. I began to shiver – I was, after all, dressed only in my hospital gown. Opposite was the funny building with steel shutters wrapped in a net. Nobody could look out of that.

Checked all the CCTV cameras were still off. Raced from the side of the buildings around the other side of the funny one. Some bushes were attempting to soften the harshness of the perimeter wall. Good cover. Behind them I ran along the wall towards the car park. I had time to wonder how any chief medical officer would know all these protocols and codes. It was a mystery to me, as was everything that had happened in the last few days.

At the car park a few people were getting into their cars to drive home at the end of the working day. Nearby was a laundry van and beside it a trolley of sheets and clothes waiting to be washed. I grabbed a green blanket and wrapped it around myself.

How was I going to get out of here? Hide inside one of these vehicles? But I was so clumsy and visible. I lurked behind a bush and watched vehicles come and go, wondering how much time I had before they would come after me. Entry and exit of vehicles through the unmanned checkpoint appeared to be by radio signal. Suddenly it occurred to me: I had the same technology and I had the protocols. I waited until there were no vehicles coming and going and then calmly walked to the exit and through it as the barrier lifted upon exchange of the correct protocols via the invisible radio link.

I was free. Possibly the first person ever to escape from the Centre for Genetic Rehabilitation. I staggered away, towards a group of trees. As I was going, I reactivated the

CCTV cameras and the locks. My mother always taught me to leave things just as you found them. And you ought to respect your mother, oughtn't you?

But something wasn't right. As my adrenaline rush subsided, my legs gave away underneath me. I tried to crawl towards some bushes, out of sight of the road, but a hammer was pounding in my head again. I collapsed on to the ground. Now the hammer was melting and turning white, spreading all over. I couldn't see the road or the bushes. What was it that was happening? What was it that was spreading? What was it spreading into? Into everything…

What was everything? Everything, what was that? What is it that is what? What is asking what is what? What? What? What doesn't know. Doesn't know nothing.

Nothing…

16. Thom Gunn

"The thing is, Julian, I don't know whether I can trust him. For all I know he's being paid by my papa to report everything I do back to him." I was whispering into Julian's ear, sitting close by his bed in his room in Salvation House, while I could see Dominic waiting outside through the window. "So if I ask him to come with me, Papa will know. But if I go without him, I risk being picked up."

I hoped I wasn't making Julian feel worse talking to him like this. I was holding his hand as he lay back against his pillows, eyes closed deep within their sockets, breathing shallowly.

"Mmmm," he groaned. "Does he… have to know… why you're going to Deptford? Make up… a cover story?"

"I don't know. I have no idea what else is in Deptford, why anyone would want to go there."

"At least you know… your mother's alive. That's good." A trace of a smile passed over his lips.

"Yeah, it's brilliant. Thanks, Julian. It's good to talk to you. Listen," I looked at him and couldn't think of much to say that was encouraging. Julian had had the virus for a long time, and it had opened him up to various infections. Now, cells were turning cancerous faster than he could be treated. "Hang in there, all right? I'll come back and let you know how it goes. Au revoir."

I kissed him and left, to find myself with Dominic again, leaning against the wall opposite the doorway, inspecting his nails. I smiled sweetly and let him follow me back towards the foyer.

Salvation House was still a hive of activity, with a stream of people coming in to check the noticeboards and talk. On a TV screen mounted on the wall, the twenty-four-hour news was showing the North Peckham estate being walled in with steel and electronics, and the reassurances that every convenience would be laid on for those inside so they would suffer no loss of quality in their lives.

An American politician was warning Britain to get things under control or they'd have to stop all trade with the country.

Cheri spotted me and came over. "We've just decided. We're going to resist forcible removal, but if the worst comes to the worst, we will move all our facilities into the Zone," she said, the words tumbling over each other with fatigue. "The only thing we can do is to be faithful to our mission. We think the whole idea of the Zone is very, very wrong. But if that's where the sufferers are, that's where we should go, don't you think? But some of the patients, like your friend Julian, can't be moved. And many of our staff won't come. They're worried they won't ever be let out."

"Why?" I asked, relieved that she wasn't angry with me any more. Events seemed to have overtaken that. "They can't keep healthy people in there as well!"

"What they're saying now is that support workers will be able to come and go with security passes, but they'll have to pass through a decontamination unit, similar to what they use for Marburg or Ebola outbreaks in Africa. Honestly, it's completely irrational. I am so furious."

"Cheri." I touched her arm. "You don't have to be Florence Nightingale."

"Someone has to do this, darling, we can't abandon people like you. How can healthy people stand by and let this happen? Are you coming on the demo tomorrow? We're expecting a hundred thousand."

"Do you think it's safe? How do you know they won't round us all up and dump us in the Zone?"

"There'll be too many of us. This is still a democracy, you know, last time I looked. They can't stop a legal protest."

"I don't know…" I trailed off. A demo might be a great place to be when you're feeling well, and not scared. But… I was shivering. I'd caught a chill. And my arm felt so sore. Besides, I had a mission…

"As the deadline approaches, they'll check on all the carers one by one. If they don't surrender their hybrids, they'll risk going to jail."

Dominic shifted uncomfortably.

"But I don't want to go! I won't be put in a prison!" I shouted.

"All the more reason to resist – come on the march. Together we can stop it!"

I heard these words but I didn't really accept their truth.

Suddenly I saw Mark, fiddling with some equipment and talking to a sound technician. I said goodbye to Cheri and went over to him.

"Mark."

He looked up at me. "Oh, Kestrella. Still talking to me, huh? Didn't think you would after we lost your friend."

"It wasn't your fault, Mark, it was ours too. We were so naive. We walked right into it."

"Have you heard anything about Johnny?"

I shook my head. "Don't expect to – ever again. That's what happens, isn't it? Did you ever hear of anybody coming out of the CGR?"

"No, but there's always a first time, you know. A change of political will could see them all released tomorrow. Actually, that's what I'm working on right now."

"What do you mean?"

He snapped shut a flight box containing his equipment and stood up, nodding to the sound technician with his microphone on a boom across his shoulder. "We're making a documentary about the pandemic. Did I tell you? We're asking a lot of tricky questions about whether what the government's up to is the correct response to the emergency. Some real facts about the prevalence of the plague and how it transmits. And the reactions of different groups. So-o, we've just been interviewing your aunt and a few other people here to get their reactions to the new emergency law. But the real coup would be if we could get to interview someone from the Hybrid Resistance Army."

My heart leapt, but I tried not to show it. "Really? Um, but how on earth did you get in touch with them? I thought they were a secret organisation?"

He laughed. "Sure, they don't want to be caught. But all protest groups want publicity. They want to get their demands across, the conditions under which they'll stop their attacks. Did you hear about their latest target?"

"No," I said. "What was it?"

"Near the proposed Zone in North Peckham. A small explosion, nobody hurt. Of course, for some of the papers it plays into their hands. Take a look at this…"

He held up the front page of a London newspaper. The headline screamed: "Hybrid terror bomb!" And underneath: "Pictures and analysis in our special Keep Britain Normal eight-page pull-out." Another paper shouted: "LOCK THEM UP!"

I didn't know what to make of it. I didn't usually read the papers. "But do you really think they should be using bombs? They might hurt innocent people. Will that really get everybody on our side?" I asked.

Mark shrugged and grinned. "That's exactly what I'd like to talk to them about, if only I could get in touch with them."

I leant forward and spoke as quietly as I could. "What if I said I knew how to do just that?"

A few minutes later, after Mark had said goodbye to his sound technician, he jumped into the car with Dominic and I, to travel through the dark streets of London back to my place.

As we drove across the city, I could see that posters had mushroomed overnight on the hoardings: "Keep Britain Normal" they roared. "Please report anything suspicious." "THE INVISIBLE ENEMY: Don't let it spread." Each screamed the Freephone number for the Biological Security Force so that citizens could betray any hybrids they saw, or in fact anyone they suspected of succumbing to the virus. Innocent flu and meningitis victims were often being reported to the Gene Police because the symptoms at the initial stage of Creep were similar.

Creep begins with a fever. I remembered when I got it; I was at school, hot flushes spread over my body and I fainted. They took me home and a rash flared on my arm. After a few days, the sores burst and began weeping. Then I went into a coma. This was the really dangerous part. Inside me a battle raged for three to four days between my immune system and the virus. The virus produced chemicals that fooled the immune system into thinking the invader was part of the body itself. When I woke up, the cells on the end of my arm were already starting to change as the virus reprogrammed the DNA in them, in a way which allowed them to incorporate non-organic elements. This is why they call that stage the rewrite. Papa and Maman cried a lot and argued between themselves for letting me use my mobile so much.

At home, I discovered a letter waiting for me. A brown envelope bore an official Home Office stamp. Its message was short and without poetry – there were even two misprints. Under the heading Biological Security Notice, it read:

You are hereby ordered, under the Emergency Powers Act, as a registered hybrid [and here was my personal ID number] *to report to Gate C on North Peckham Estate* [there was a map] *at* [and here was the time and date – four weeks hence]. *Please be prompt in order to void queues. Bring with you any personnel belongings that will fit into one 30 kilo bag. Bring all relevant documentation. Failure to attend will result in your arrest and a £250,000 fine.*

The printed signature was that of Hunter Cracke himself.

Mark told me that throughout the whole country, there were an estimated 15,000 Greys and 8000 Blues. Most of the Blues would do what they were told and move into the Zone, either because they believed it was for the best or because their carers would insist. Nobody knew what the Greys would do of course, but there was a lot of talk on the net about them congregating in the more remote parts of the country, in Wales, Cornwall or Scotland.

"If you wanted to go there, I could make it happen," Mark offered.

"I'll think about it," I said.

Papa emerged from his quarters, fresh from a shower. "They're not going to take my daughter into the Zone," he said when he saw the letter, and I felt a flush of pleasure. "I will find somewhere to hide you."

He tried calling his friends in Paris who had a private jet, but they were hesitant about getting involved. He called friends in Yorkshire and the Cotswolds, owners of large houses secure in their own grounds where he thought I might be safe. One made excuses about having to go away, the other had the decorators in. Before he embarrassed anyone else I told him not to bother or he soon wouldn't have any friends left. "It's better for me to accept my fate," I said.

Mark was filming the whole thing and Papa was so preoccupied that he hadn't taken much notice. So Mark thought he'd try his luck. "By the way, you wouldn't agree to being interviewed, would you?" he asked.

"Ah, no," my father politely declined. "I'm afraid it's company policy that all questions have first to be screened by the media relations department. Besides," he added, "I rather think any question you would be allowed to ask me you would already know the answer to."

"But," said Mark, "you're the company's media relations department boss."

"Exactly," he murmured. "This is why I speak with such authority."

Mark smiled. "I don't suppose you can point me in the direction of any cures on the horizon, interesting lines of research?"

"Mark," he said courteously. "As soon as there are, you will be the first to know."

I had always admired Papa. He was elegant, clearly very important, and he must be good at his job to earn such a fabulous amount of money. I still admired him, but I was beginning to see exactly where his loyalties lay. And I found myself wondering how far those loyalties extended into the rest of his life.

Soon he disappeared to catch up with his paperwork. Having seen me home, Dominic had also departed on his night off. That left Mark and I alone, able to talk freely. I explained about the letters I'd found, and Thom Gunn, and what Maman had said about the bombing, and then what "an informant" had told me about how to find the HRA – I didn't want to get Julian into trouble.

Mark gaped. "That is amazing. Your mother.... the model..." I could see the way his mind was working. What a scoop it would be to run the story that the famous ex-model was now a hybrid terrorist.

"Mark, you mustn't mention my mother. Promise me. Not without first meeting her and getting her permission at any rate."

I could see a sense of responsibility calming his features as he realised he had to play this by the book. "Of course, of course, Kestrella. I owe you a big favour after all. But now you're doing me one. Just tell me where to go and I'll take it from there."

I then played my ace card. "But Mark, don't you think it would make great television if I were to interview Thom Gunn?"

"You? Why?"

"As a hybrid – daughter of the disappeared ex-model and charity worker who is a member of their group – sceptical of the violence – a voice for peace and negotiation."

I could see him thinking this through. "Yes. Yes, that would be perfect. If he'll agree to it."

"He's met Cheri, my aunt." I explained how he saved Sally House from the vigilantes. "Those attackers would have burnt the place down if he hadn't turned up."

"Ri-ight." Cogs were moving fast in Mark's brain. "I can see I've got a night's work ahead of me. It all hinges on whether your lead plays out. Just tell me where to go."

"An amusement arcade called The Soft Machine, somewhere in Deptford. Ask for Thom Gunn." I hoped Julian's information was still right.

"I'm on my way now. If I'm lucky it might still be open." Mark headed briskly for the door, winking at me. "I'll call you tomorrow!" was his parting shot. "Thanks a lot, Kestrella!"

I couldn't get to sleep that night. I finally dozed off properly at seven only to be woken by the phone an hour later. I leapt on it thinking it was Mark. But it was Cheri.

"Kestrella, I have some sad news. Julian passed away during the night. I'm very sorry."

I felt terribly upset and subdued. Poor, poor Julian. He did so believe he would live. He tried so hard. But the virus never stopped creeping, until it had totally saturated him. Was that what was in store for me? For all of us? When Mark did call I guess I didn't sound as enthusiastic as he expected when he told me the news.

"I met Gunn and he's totally up for it. It's fantastic, thank you so much, Kestrella. Can you be at the Crick and Watson Hotel in Waterloo in three hours?"

Three hours…

Still groggy, I turned up at a cheap two-star hotel on a neglected back street. It was really little more than a crash pad run by the Turkish mother of a hybrid who was stuck to a tacky, portable Space Invaders game that had long since broken. Both were sympathetic to the HRA cause, which was why they were letting Gunn and Mark use it for this purpose, provided there were no clues to the location in the final piece. Mother and son formed a sad duo behind the reception desk.

But Dominic was on the other end of my lead again. I had yet to shake him off if my plan to find my mother had a chance of working without Papa finding out.

In the greasy foyer Mark persuaded Dominic to wait in a café across the road. There was no room for him either in the room where the interview was to take place – or in the whole cramped hotel.

"Trust me, I'm a documentary maker!" Mark gave Dominic his best smile.

Dominic agreed, on condition that Mark promised to bring me right back within two hours. He walked over to the Portuguese café opposite to do what he did best, leaving me to breathe a sigh of relief.

Mark and I climbed upstairs. The carpet was worn, the paintwork chipped, the furniture looked as if it would collapse if you sat on it. There was a stale animal smell which I couldn't identify.

As he showed me into the bedroom which they were using for the interview, I saw that Mark had set his camera up so that his subject would be in silhouette, in front of the window facing the door.

This was how I first saw Thom Gunn. He was immediately identifiable by the shape of his rifle and his large build. The lighting cameraman turned the lights on and I saw him properly. He was a powerfully built black youth, two metres tall. He stared directly and insolently at me, chewing gum and grinning as if he thought he knew something I didn't – no doubt about my mother.

"Hiya. Don't think I've had the pleasure," he said, holding his hand out as Mark introduced us. His grip enclosed my right hand like a bear's paw and he held it longer than he needed to, pulling me nearer to him so he could look at my other arm and see the phone. "All right, that's cool," he drawled in a mid-Atlantic accent that I thought sounded so fake, like he'd modelled himself on some rap singer. "Hey, you know we've got a few of those. You'd be in good company if you joined us, Kes. Meet a few of your own kind. None of us going into that Zone, no way, get it?" He sat down again, spreading his legs wide apart. My hand tingled for a while after he had let go. But his eyes never left mine.

"We're just finishing setting up," said Mark. "Then we're ready to shoot."

Gunn cheered, waving his rifle in the air as if he thought making a pun on the word shoot was funny. Mark pulled up a chair for me opposite Gunn's. I had dressed in an expensive, tight sweater of a shade that matched my eyes, tied my hair back and spent an hour on make-up. I now felt more exposed to Gunn's hungry gaze than I'd thought I would feel from Mark's camera. I didn't like the way he was looking at me. Maybe I should have worn something different. I tried to appear relaxed, but inside I felt shredded.

The cramped bedroom was crowded with, besides us, the second lighting cameraman and a sound guy, the bed pushed to one side. But soon they were ready to film from two angles in such a way that we were both silhouetted the whole time to conceal our appearance. Mark began by asking us some questions about the firebombing.

I took the position of being against any violence and in favour of the Quarantine Zone because I wanted to argue against this man who had stolen my mother from me. I told Gunn I'd willingly go in the Zone if I thought it would save all the healthy people, like my father and Cheri. Didn't Gunn have any loved ones he wanted to protect?

He sneered at me. "'Course I do, but this ain't the way to save them."

I asked him if he thought violence would win people over to his side.

"We don't wanna hurt nobody," he said. "Our actions give us a platform to say what we think and have people listen. Ain't that what most terrorism is about? 'Cept the sort that kills innocent civilians. We'd never do that. We're no suicide bombers. Wasn't Nelson Mandela called a terrorist? They're often called terrorists until they've won approval and then they're called freedom fighters. If there was another way, don't you think we'd choose it?"

I replied that I didn't think the end justified the means, and that if you wanted to keep the moral high ground, then you shouldn't stoop to the same level as your enemies. Then he hit me below the belt.

"And what about your mum, Kes?"

"Wh–what do you mean…?"

"If she was missing and the Gene Police had taken her, wouldn't you do anything to get her back?"

I stared at him. I knew he knew about Maman and also that he knew that I knew it. He was playing a game with me and I hated it. Suddenly I was on my feet, screaming. "How dare you! How dare you! Don't you bring Maman into this!" I found myself ineffectually kicking his legs, but he just sat there grinning at me like a hyena.

"What about it, Kes? Would you join us if it got her back?" he challenged.

"No! Not if you were the last people on earth," I spat.

"Woh!" Mark put down his camera. "Cut, er, I guess, folks." He stared at me, as I panted heavily. "You OK, Kestrella?" he asked.

I turned away into the lights before they had dimmed and found myself blinded temporarily. As I was swaying, eyes shut, Gunn took my hand before I could stop him and whispered into my ear. "Hey, Kes," he said. I didn't like the way he shortened my name. Only Maman was allowed to do that – had he heard Maman say it? "We both know what this is really about. Why don't you come back to my place after this and I'll show you around? No commitment, no risk, promise." He leant closer and whispered. "How 'bout it?"

I pulled my hand away, forced my eyes open and met his gaze full on, struggling with my feelings. Of course this is what I wanted, but I didn't want to make him think that if I did, it was because I liked him. But he could see which way I was leaning. His face broke into a grin.

"'At's it, babe!" he turned to Mark. "You guys through?"

Mark looked up from his laptop, where he was viewing the footage. "Think so. Can I contact you if there's a problem?"

"Sure thing. You know where to find me, don't you? See ya then." He grabbed my good hand again and started to pull me to the door. "Let's go. No time like the present, eh?"

"Sure you're OK, Kestrella?" I heard Mark call behind me as we sneaked down the stairs.

"Yes, thanks, Mark!" I shouted. "Bye!"

Gunn guided me out of the rear exit to avoid Dominic, with a nod to the Turkish proprietess. In the back alley, an unmarked white van waited. Gunn hustled me in the back, jumped in after and closed the door. It was pitch-black and as the van lurched away it threw me on to him. How embarrassing. I couldn't help letting loose a little scream and immediately regretted it.

Be strong, I told myself. You're not a little girl any more.

17. The dump at the end of the world

The first sensations... Pains, fading in like a piece of music. A rhythm section, bass and drums, was a dull ache in the back of my head that echoed down my neck to duet with the throbbing in my limbs. A piercing trumpet shrieked sore notes of free-form jazz. Aggressive slashes of stringed instruments, piercing attacks of stabbing bows and the whine of high-pitched oboes were my inflamed, burning nerves, pinched tissues and tinnitus screaming in my ears.

Some of them played on the surface of my skin, others in the muscle tissue or the joints, and still more, the really deep dull ones, reverberated in the marrowed tunnels of my bones.

Somehow, as I became more conscious, I remembered this as being familiar: I seemed to have been here before.

But that's all I could recall – the feeling of remembering, remembering pain.

I opened my eyes to see people staring at me. Although they were talking, I couldn't understand what they were saying. It was clear they knew me. But they were wary and arguing about what to do with me. I looked around: a small space crammed with clutter; a vehicle, the type you could live in on the road.

Now I became aware of another sensation – thirst and hunger. I tried to speak, but for some reason I couldn't, so I reached up to point at my mouth to indicate my thirst. I was shocked to touch something cold and hard. With my hands I explored where my face should be and found something smooth and plastic. A feeling of immense disappointment and sadness overtook me. I felt betrayed, as if I was the butt of some stupid joke. I realised I'd only thought I'd opened my eyes and that in fact I didn't have any eyes to open. I was seeing through something else.

But, noticing my actions, two of these people knew what to do. They took a tube hanging down from my neck and stuck it in a bottle of brown liquid. After some experimentation I found I was able to suck, and felt it sliding into my stomach… a snake of nectar bringing reconnection to the world. Yes, I'd done this before, many times. It wasn't normal for other people but for some reason it was for me. I was special.

But I was very tired. I drifted away, and when I came back to the pain and the disappointment again, I felt another sensation – motion. The van was trundling over a bumpy surface. Someone was holding my hand and that felt good. It was a girl wearing baggy clothing. Neither of us spoke. After a while the van pulled up and she opened the door.

"You know how to walk, don't you?" she said.

I sat up, twisted around and tried my feet on the floor. That felt OK so I stood up. I put weight on them and stumbled. But, yes, I was able to walk if I held on to something. I stepped out.

Piles of rubbish greeted me, as far as could be seen. Why had they brought me here? Was this my home?

The sky was grey, but it must have been late in the day for the light was fading. Gradually, figures emerged from the shadows to approach the van. Three people had accompanied me and they greeted the figures. The girl turned to me and said: "I think you'll be safer here among people like you than you would be with us. It's a shame you couldn't tell us how you escaped. Perhaps your memory will come back. Remember, your name is Johnny. I'm sorry we don't know anything more about you. We'll come back sometimes to see how you are. Bye bye."

I watched as they climbed back into the van and it drove off to be swallowed by the dusty gloom.

I turned to stare at my new companions. With wild and feral looks in their eyes, those whose eyes I could see, they dripped wires and pieces of broken gadgetry, and their clothes were made of whatever they could find and bind together with wires and tape. They regarded me with suspicion. One of them, who was carrying a long metal pole with coloured rags hanging off each end, came up to me. He was tall and gaunt, with a bandanna round his head and a scar down his face. He peered closely at my screen and tapped it with the end of his staff. I didn't react. He pushed me backwards, and when I still didn't react, he pushed me more aggressively and started to yell. I wasn't sure what to do. I tripped on something and fell over, and he started to kick me. So I grabbed hold of his legs and pulled him down. We started struggling on the floor. He had the neck of a bass guitar sticking out of his jacket and I grabbed hold of it and yanked and he howled like a madman. He dug his fingernails into the transition at the side of my head. The pain was excruciating.

Instinctively, I kicked him in the balls, picked up a rock and aimed it at his head but he blocked the move, pushed me back and knelt with one leg pinning me down and his staff across my neck. He was about to use a rock to smash my screen when somebody grabbed it off him.

This guy was shorter and stockier and had the neck of an electric guitar sticking out of his clothes. There was a scuffle and much shouting. The pair of them rolled over and over down a slope, through a puddle, into a pile of rubbish. The small crowd of other ragbag hybrids began to cheer. After a few minutes of pointless grappling and grunting they separated, and the tall one backed off, growling, before any real damage was done to him. The other got up and walked towards me, dusting himself down.

"Hm. Name's Slash. What's yours?"

"Johnny – I think," I replied. "But I guess I've lost my memory. Where the hell am I?"

"Lost your memory?" replied Slash. "You're in a bloody mess that's where you are." And he started to laugh. "You're at the end of the world, mate."

Then he turned to face the others who were watching. "All right, you lot, sod off, party's over." The crowd dispersed, mumbling to itself. Slash guided me away to a nearby makeshift hut constructed from pallets and plastic sheets. Inside were some tin drums for seats and a crate for a table.

"This is my shed," he said. "They won't bother you in here."

We sat down and talked. Slash began to explain that everybody here was a creature on the edge, scavenging an existence in the back of beyond – a landfill tip in the wilderness east of London where nobody else could live. "Everybody here is pretty much like you," he said. "They all want to forget their past cos it's too much pain. You're lucky – you really have lost your memory. We all got new names here – Wirey, Plasma, Knobs, Twiddle, Speaker, Trash an' that. We better call you something – how 'bout... I dunno – Pixelface?"

Pixelface. I shrugged. It was as good as anything. "Who was that other guy, the one who attacked me?" I asked.

"That's Metal Gristle," said Slash. "A real psycho."

"He is totally gone," I agreed. My head still smarted where he'd scraped at my sores.

"There's about thirty of us. Every now and then someone new turns up or someone dies. Me, I been here a few months. I remember what it was like at first – I didn't have a clue. So stick with me for a few days and I'll show you what's what," he offered.

Over the next few days Slash showed me the ropes. We lived off the rubbish; whenever the lorries came to dump it, we hid. As soon as they left, we rushed out to see what they'd brought, picking through the festering produce thrown out by the markets and restaurants of London. I suppose our diet was balanced – a bit of everything – English, Chinese, Italian, often perfectly good fruit and vegetables. The real problem was fresh water. It had to be carried in plastic drums from a public toilet two miles away. We could have been living on the edge of a sprawling African shanty town.

I managed by not thinking. Nobody talked about their past. I didn't care. I had no past to talk about.

Somebody had invented a name for us bunch of scavenging losers: the Flotsam. Each of us alone in their own lost world. There was a certain camaraderie. We'd enjoy sharing a good haul – a sack of ripe mandarins, boxes of overripe mushrooms – or collecting wood to make fire. But that went out the window as soon as something desirable turned up and there wasn't enough to go around. A fight would break out. I stayed well out of these – it meant nothing to me. Usually, Metal Gristle would be the winner because he wasn't afraid to smash somebody's legs or skull if he felt like it. Perhaps some of the lorry drivers caught glimpses of us, but if so they didn't seem to give a damn. We were invisible.

Sometimes at night we sat around making music. The ones that were musical instruments like Slash and Metal Gristle played them and the rest of us made a racket banging on tin drums, blocks of wood, whatever.

Sometimes people found alcohol: unfinished bottles of wine or spirits. They'd slip some in my bottle. We'd get high and dance round the campfire in the pouring rain howling like the mad animals we almost were. At times like this, I could forget my name and the pain again. Afterwards, the others would grow weepy and whine about their childhood, their mothers and fathers and all that stuff they no longer had, and I was glad I didn't have any of that.

Some of them used drugs – anything they could find, which wasn't much: spirits, solvents or glue. I just watched them stumbling around, jabbering at things that weren't there, and felt some kind of envy. Sometimes, when they got high, some of them would attack their hybrid parts, trying to rip out the wiring, the plastic, the metal, any part that wasn't human, because they hated it so much. If only they could be human again, they could get back to the world they came from. But they might as well have been trying to pull their own legs off. In the morning, when they came to and realised what they'd done, their screams were so loud they were probably heard in the East End of London.

On such a night as this Metal Gristle decided to have a go at me again. This time Slash wasn't around to help. He was sick, groaning in his hut. The rain was coming down without mercy and had been for three days. The plastic over our shanty town shacks was not much defence against this kind of onslaught and putrid, toxic rivers ran through our yard, under the walls and beneath the pallets we slept on. What light there was came from my face and that of a girl called Games, plus a few other gizmos like that. Gristle had gone outside and when he came back he decided I was sitting on his chair.

"Get off," he ordered.

But it wasn't his seat and I wasn't going to move. So he pushed me off. He'd been goading me like this ever since I arrived and I was fed up with it. This time I hit back. He roared with delight. He liked it when people fought back. The rest of the pack was scared of him and never did it. But he and I were the same height and I wasn't scared – I had nothing to lose. I lashed out and connected with his jaw. He swung a fist at me and hit the side of my screen, which jarred all the way down my neck and spine. I kicked out at his shin. He howled, then brought both hands down on the back of my skull. The rest of the pack was cheering and had made a space for us in the centre. We locked into each other and I pushed him against a table. We collapsed on to the floor and rolled over and over, dislodging bottles and cans and getting soaked. Whenever he rolled over the neck of his guitar it was agony for him and I played this to my advantage. His teeth sank into my arm where the keyboard was. "Why are you doing this?" I kept saying. "If you stop, so will I. I don't want to fight you, but if you insist I can kill you."

After a couple of minutes of this I was really suffering, and I guessed he was too. He was bleeding from his cheek and my head was screaming from where he kept bashing my screen. He'd drawn blood on my arm and I was wondering whether my keyboard would ever work again. But he was in a worse state. He could barely stand up. The crowd was chanting, urging us to finish the job – they wanted one of us done for. I managed to grab hold of Metal Gristle's metal bar and twist it out of his grip. I knocked him down and had brought the bar up ready to smash it on to his head. The crowd yelled for blood.

I could see there was no more fight in him. An imperceptible shake of his head. A dulling of the light in his eyes. I threw the bar aside and walked away to the far corner. Some of the others crowded around me to congratulate me, but I wasn't interested. Games gave me water, which I drank gratefully.

After a while I went back over to Gristle. He was nursing his wounds.

"You OK?" I asked.

He nodded.

"Why'd you do it? I kept saying I didn't want to fight."

"I got to."

"Why you got to, Gristle?"

"Dunno," he managed. "Cos it hurts." It was obviously an effort for him to admit this.

"What hurts, Gristle?" I said as gently as I could manage.

"Back. At back." And he pointed at the base of his spine.

"Here?" I asked. He nodded. "Mind if I take a look?"

He shook his head. Nobody else was watching. They were all playing a game around the table which they'd reassembled. He lifted up the various layers of what passed for clothing and I was able to see by the light of my monitor that his skin was in a terrible state. I saw that the bass guitar was sticking out of his side, but that wasn't where the problem was. A couple of strings from the neck were disappearing into his spine. It was clear that whenever he moved around they tore against the skin and dug into it. The wound was infected.

"Stay there," I said.

I went looking for something to cut the wire with. I came back with a tin can lid and proceeded to saw into the wire until I could break first one and then the other. It didn't take long. That took the pressure off. I then cleaned the wound. Gristle could feel the benefit of the release straight away and stretched in a direction he hadn't reached for many months.

He turned around with an expression of gratitude on his face I'd never seen before. "Thanks, mate," he said and held out his hand. I shook it. "I feel better already."

From that moment on we were friends. His temper had gone because the pain had gone. I don't know why he could never admit it to anyone before. Maybe he didn't know himself. Anyway, after that, the rest of the Flotsam thought of me as their leader. They started bringing their own problems to me to solve. Hardware, software, health. Like I was some kind of miracle worker.

There were hardly any tools. One Torx screwdriver that only fitted half the gadgets, and one Phillips, all that was left of a full set of attachments for a guy called

Driller, whose arm ended in a power tool. I fixed a broken casing, rewired an amp, applied crude dressings to wounds, soldered connections using a coat-hanger and a fire, and treated infections with lemons and yogurt that had been dumped the day before. I had no idea how I knew what to do. Sometimes it worked. But there was loads I couldn't do, so I tried to get us to work things out together. Like organise ourselves.

The next day the rain stopped and the sun pushed weakly through. I started some of them on building duty, repairing the shacks. I set up a rota so there were no longer arguments about whose turn it was to fetch water, prepare food or wash up. People could see it was fair and there was a certain amount of relief. The mood changed. I got people digging trenches so that the putrid water never came through the campsite again. We found containers and cleaned them and used them for collecting rainwater. And life became very slightly less hellish.

From time to time the people who had brought me here would come back. They would ask me how I was and bring news. They told me about how they'd met me once before when I'd visited them. Apparently, I'd brought friends with me: a beautiful young girl and a man around thirty with a video camera. They said I ought to try and remember who I was. They said I must be very clever because I'd escaped from the CGR and nobody had ever done that before. When the Flotsam heard this, I was even more of a hero. Respect.

"Hey. Maybe you can help us escape from here to a better place one day, Pixelface," Slash chipped in hopefully.

I was told I was a computer and that was probably why I was rational and good at organising. And that my memory banks had been wiped as I escaped.

They suggested I try to put my memory together. I wasn't sure if this was a good idea. I feared my keyboard wouldn't work after Metal Gristle had bitten into it. But surprisingly it did – it had begun to heal itself just as if it were part of my body.

Gingerly, I began to explore inside. Only a handful of files on my internal hard disk had escaped from whatever happened at the CGR. Many were just fragments left over after the rest had been destroyed, like charred scraps of paper burnt in a fire. When I couldn't open certain files, I deciphered others until I found passwords that let me open them. Slowly, my knowledge grew.

It wasn't like remembering. It was like reading about somebody else. I supposed I must have been this person who referred to himself as Johnny Online, but it was a stupid name and he was an unhappy, twisted person. I preferred being Pixelface, a boy with no past.

I was unaware that my efforts were severely hampered by the absence of Internet at the landfill site. I only knew what I found within myself: a wired, overstrung, plastic spastic, a faceless, graceless, mechanised fossil. Such crusty body armour must mean I had a heart of silicon, a metal mind inflexible as pitted steel. No wonder I'd ended up here on the edge of the known world, in the place where everything unwanted was thrown away. With all these other useless, pointless things – rotten, putrid rubbish.

18. The Hybrid Resistance Army

I was huddled up in a corner of the pitch blackness, sitting on an old tyre and gripping a rail down the side of the van to stop from being hurled about whenever we rent round a corner.

Suddenly I felt Gunn's hand on my leg. "Stay still," he whispered. I tried to pull my leg away, but he was too strong. "Don't struggle. Or you'll get hurt."

"What are you doing?" I panicked. He was big, and muscular. He could do anything to me.

"You wanna see your mother don't you?" he hissed.

"Yes, but—"

"Then you have to co-operate."

He had moved up close now and I could feel his hand pulling up the legs of my jeans.

"Get off!" I yelled.

"Relax, will you?" The barrel of his rifle against my

other leg stilled me. "I gotta do this, or there's no way I'm taking you to our HQ."

"Leave me alone – I'll tell my mother when I see her!"

"Oh, I'm sure she'd approve," he responded.

"You're mad!" I shouted.

"You're the one who's crazy. Anyone'd think I was trying to rape you."

"Well, what are you trying to do?"

"Take your tag off, of course. Where is it?" He was feeling up and down my legs. "Ah."

Before I could object, something cold and metallic had slipped underneath it, pulled back sharply – and it fell away. It happened so fast there was nothing I could do.

"How – how dare you do that without asking!" I gasped, breathing heavily.

I heard him snort in the darkness. There was a flash of light as he quickly opened the back of the van and threw the tag out. I had time to see the little thing bounce a couple of times on the road before he slammed the door shut again. That tiny band had been almost a part of me for so long. I rubbed my skin where it had been. It felt strange and exposed. I had stopped thinking of the tag as horrible, even though it was; it was something that kept me safe, kept me from being whisked off to the CGR. It had allowed me to stay at home with Papa and have big, strong Dominic look after me, however much I resented him. As long as it was there, I could pretend things were relatively normal. Pretend.

And with one easy action, Gunn had ripped that away from me. I started to cry.

"Hey, Kes…" whispered Gunn. He touched me again, this time on the shoulder.

"Get off me!" I screamed. And this time he did.

"OK…"

All I could think was that now they'd be after me. They'd soon find out that I was no longer wearing it. They'd send out a van. Ten vans. I'd be caught and sent away. I'd never see Papa again.

"I thought it was what you wanted…" said Gunn. "You must've realised you couldn't come with me while you were wearing it. They'd track you. It would jeopardise our whole operation."

No. I hadn't realised. Another thing I hadn't thought through. I'd really burnt my bridges now. He handed me a tissue. I blew my nose.

"Come on. It ain't so bad. Where you're going, we're all Greys. You'll be in good company. And we're nearly there now."

The van turned left suddenly, banging me against the side again, and lurched to a halt. Outside I heard Alsatians barking their heads off. The engine cut. I heard a heavy gate clang shut behind us and bolts being shot. The back door was flung open and light streamed in to show me the man with the rifle for an arm smiling his impossibly wide smile. To me, he looked like a wolf.

"Kes, hey, relax. Let's get out."

Gunn jumped down and swung round to offer me his free hand all in one fluid movement. Slowly, I emerged, looking round into a muddy, oily yard strewn with scrap metal and disembowelled cars. I saw we'd come through a tall steel gate set in a barbed-wire topped iron fence. Down one side of the yard were a low brick building with a corrugated roof and a few sheds.

Gunn was sauntering around, arms outstretched. "Scrappie," he grinned. "Makes a good cover. Ironic too, don'cha think? Spare parts… recycling… unwanted scrap… and us. Rejected, recycled… But the future of the human race. I have no doubt 'bout that. Isn't that why they're trying to wipe us out?"

He gestured with his rifle towards the building and its flaky green door. On his face was the trace of a cheeky smile. Suddenly my whole mood changed. I kept my eyes on the green door as I ran towards it and opened it and looked around a small dark workshop to see Maman sitting at a table smiling at me.

When I'd had my fill of crying and being hugged and repeating that I thought I'd never see her again, I withdrew from her arms to feast my eyes upon her.

"Oh, my darling! You found me!" she murmured. "You're so clever!"

"You look different," I replied. She seemed more raw, less polished. Of course, she wasn't wearing make-up and she probably hadn't washed her hair in her usual shampoo and conditioner all this time. "There's something in your eyes … and the way you're holding yourself." A model is always used to posing even when she's not working. Although Maman hadn't been one for a couple of years and had played the part of the head of a charity in the public eye, she'd always maintained her character armour – her outward façade. But now it had gone.

"Do you think so, *ma chérie*?" she said, smiling at me. "Better, I hope!"

But my relief was changing into something else. "You left. Without saying a word! Why? Didn't you trust me?"

She sat back to observe me with half a smile playing over her face. I knew that expression: weighing up in her mind the proportion of child versus adult in me at this point in my life, and therefore the correct dosage of information to impart to me. As if information were a medicine that had to be meted out according to the age of the recipient. She took a deep breath and said: "I know. I should have told you. But there was no time. I always knew I could write to you. Didn't you get my letters?"

I told her how I had discovered her letters hidden away by Papa, about Johnny and everything, and it made me cry once more. As I did so, I was embarrassingly aware of Gunn coming into the room.

"That confirms what I feared," she said, growing darker and more distant. "Your father hates me – and wanted to use you against me. *Zut!* I should have known."

Gunn came over, and to my horror, he squeezed her shoulder and they took each other's hand. It made me squirm inside.

Gunn said: "Kes, girl, it's time to face facts. Your Papa is a bad man. We-ell, maybe not him. You could be kind and argue he's caught up in somethin' larger than he can handle, a rollercoaster of a project. But, you know, he could jump ship if he wanted."

"I don't believe it!" I cried. "And I can't understand why you want to be here… I gestured around the stained walls, the shelves full of old tins and oily papers, last year's tyre calendar, twenty-year-old office furniture and cracked lino "…instead of at home in the luxury you're used to – and without me! Maman, tell me the truth."

She took a deep breath again. "All right, *ma chérie*. What

I have to say may come as something of a shock. So please wait until I've finished before asking questions."

She was leaning forward and holding the wrist of my left arm, subconsciously stroking the area where I ceased to be human and became technology, just like Papa had done. Her large blue eyes stared into mine through her long eyelashes.

"I decided I couldn't live with your father any more. No, not because he was horrible to me, unless you count being away from home so much that I hardly saw him from one month to the next. But because of what I found out. I did love him, I did think he was a wonderful man, and in many ways he is. But there is another side to him, one that you don't know about. I didn't know about it until recently. You see, I realised that nobody reaches a position of power in a big company like that without making compromises. Yes, I know it's just a drug company, but it's one of the biggest in the world.

"Several years ago, Mu-Tech decided on a great scheme to make lots of money for its shareholders. For years, medical companies had been inventing so-called conditions so they could sell us a cure – things like Sudden Panic Syndrome or the cure for laziness. But they ran out of ideas. Their profits were sliding. So they decided to do the ultimate thing and create a disease for which they already had the cure."

She paused to make sure I was listening. "Yes, you guessed it; it was Creep. The plague was created by Papa's company."

I couldn't contain myself any longer. "But that's ridiculous! They'd have to be insane. Besides you said they had the cure! Where is it then? Why haven't they given it to us?"

"Because it doesn't work!" Maman answered. "They reckoned without the power of the virus to mutate. Once out there it developed unpredictable qualities. It evolved in response to other drugs and people's immune systems. Then, of course, they couldn't say they already had the cure for the original form because that would be admitting they knew about the disease beforehand. And how could they if they hadn't created it?"

"And Papa knows this? Is that what you're saying?"

"He's on the board. How could he not know?"

"But how can you be sure?" I said.

Gunn slapped a file on the table. "I got the evidence. Secret minutes from board meetings. Business plans, financial records. All that stuff."

"Thom came to the office of my charity," said Maman. "He said he knew I was a nice person – I must be or I wouldn't have started my charity. But he said if I really cared about drug victims, the Creep issue was far greater than that of the fashion models I was trying to help. He told me what I've just told you. I didn't believe him either until he showed me the evidence. He said it came from a whistle-blower inside Mu-Tech. He wanted me to confront Papa. With him of course. But first I thought it was better if I left and joined him and the others. I really feel I'm needed here."

"The others?"

"There are a few of us, but not many," she continued. "Now that things are getting a lot worse, we expect our numbers to swell."

"A resistance army," said Gunn. "A Hybrid Resistance Army." He held up the rifle that was his arm. "I was in the army cadets. Been training since I was ten – my dad was in the army too. We did target practice together. Hence this."

It was all too much. I got up and started pacing around. "*Non! C'est fou!*"

Gunn took my arm. "Why d'you think there's no cure? Isn't it obvious?" I pulled free. "They're waiting until there's millions of victims and then they'll make a killing. And the politicians – don't you think they're on the board too? Everyone's been bought off. Why do you think they're introducing such measures?"

I said, "They've told me to go to the Quarantine Zone."

"Tell me you won't go!" Maman said. "You must stay here with me. I've missed you so much."

"I don't know, I don't know…" I wanted to be with her. But I hadn't expected this.

"Stay and fight, Kes. Like yer mum says!"

I wanted to change the subject. "Is this where you live?" I asked.

Gunn opened a door at the back of the room. Behind was a small cupboard. He did something and a panel came away from the back. He threw a switch and a dim light revealed a hidden room with bunk beds – and on the beds several kids a couple of years younger than me. They looked up when they saw me, blinking like a litter of kittens born in a laundry cupboard. I was introduced to them one by one – a couple of mobile phone hybrids like me, a robotic pet, a thigh toning system for heaven's sake, a mobile media centre, three games machines and two computers – but they didn't have monitors like Johnny. There was a poker game, a microwave and a power tool. They regarded me with a mixture of anticipation and shyness.

"Meet Gaynor and Peter, Kestrella," said my mum, introducing me to the mobile phone and media centre, who were closer to my age. "I think you'll get on with them."

I sat down on a chair.

"Kes—" began Gunn.

But Maman put her hand on his arm. "I think it's all a bit much for her. Leave her for a while."

I stared at the children. "They're so young, Maman. Is this really your army?"

She looked to Gunn, who answered: "No, there's more. You'll find out. Sure they're young. Most hybrids are. You know what the latest is? It's something else the government is keeping from us."

"No, but I suppose you'll tell me," I said. I was beginning to weary of all this conspiracy stuff.

"They think adolescence is a factor in getting Creep. Something about hormones and the body changing – the virus takes advantage of it to get into the cells and alter them."

I stared glumly at the grey wall. That would explain things. I'd noticed that whenever I had a period the soreness flared up. Or maybe this was nothing to do with it. But I couldn't think of anybody who was a hybrid who wouldn't have been a teenager when they caught the disease, apart from Maman. Puberty could be the catalyst. When we can start to make babies that pass our genes on. This was the cue for the virus to step in and change our genes forever.

Gaynor and Peter had come over to stand in front of me and were staring at my left arm. Gaynor held out her phone alongside mine, silently, as if to compare them or as a gesture of solidarity. She had a more recent model than mine, but just as many blisters. I gave her some of my cream which she rubbed in eagerly and passed to Peter.

Peter's media system was a wrist-strap model, and sores spread up his arm beneath his shirt sleeve. He didn't say a word and it occurred to me that he was deaf as well, as silently he displayed a slideshow of his family on the little screen: kid sister skateboarding, dad and mum fooling around by the seaside.

Maman was stroking my hair, grooming me like monkeys are supposed to do when they've been apart for a while. This felt almost normal – like we were back home and none of this had ever happened. I'd found my mother, but she'd left her home, never, I guessed, to return. So where did that leave me?

I thought about Johnny and ached. I longed for him to talk this over with. Even though I hadn't known him long I believed I could trust him with anything. I wondered what tortures he might be enduring because of me, or even if he was still alive. If I ever saw him again, I'd never rest till I'd made it up for him. Then I thought of poor Julian. A wave of tiredness overcame me. I lay down on one of the bunks and immediately fell into a deep sleep…

The next day when I got up, there was no one else in the room. I noticed a door at the back I hadn't seen last night and went through it, following the sound of voices. A crowded space like the canteen at school greeted me, and I rubbed my eyes sleepily. All the kids were in the middle of breakfast, jabbering away. Gaynor noticed and came over to guide me to where I could get some cereal and sit down at her table.

"More of us be along later, Kes," she said a couple of times.

"There must be at least fifty more altogether across London, and then there's all the normal sympathisers. Lots more than will come out and admit it cos they're frightened of what their neighbours would do to 'em. You know some people's homes've been burnt down?"

I grunted and concentrated on stuffing myself. I was wildly hungry.

Maman entered the room. Without seeing me she went up to Gunn's side and he put his arm around her shoulder and gave it a squeeze. She didn't even blink. I couldn't believe it. How could she let him do that? I turned away in disgust. Gaynor was rabbiting on.

"The lorry — we call it the School Bus — be back soon.

It goes around picking hybrids up and bringing 'em here for training, you'll see," she continued, eager to commit her enthusiasm to me. She obviously worshipped Gunn. "'Ave you seen 'is eyes?!" she giggled. "And 'is muscles!"

"How come the Gene Police don't stop it?" I asked.

"The whole place is hidden behind a recyclin' business," she explained. "The lorries that go out are collectin' scrap metal an' that. We hide in the back. No one'd guess!"

"The owner's totally into it," chipped in Peter. "That's his son over there…" He pointed at one of the games-machine kids: a fat, spotty boy in a lurid tracksuit. He was absorbed in playing on his console. No one else was paying him any attention.

"Our drill rooms are behind the company's warehouse and offices," continued Gaynor. I was more interested in watching Maman. She was checking on all the children one by one, making sure they were OK, smiling and giving them little hugs and strokes. I suddenly thought how like Aunt Cheri she had become. Each of them had taken on their own brood of misfits to care for and make them feel wanted. Why? Did Maman care for them more than she cared for me?

Gunn was fond of giving speeches. When everyone had finished eating, he stood and silenced the racket of banter and arguments by banging on the table with his rifle. He began to paint a vision of a country that was tolerant of difference, that embraced the future without fear and that took care of those less fortunate. "As you all know, fear breeds fear!" he said passionately. "And fear is caused by unfamiliarity and ignorance. It's only because there's no cure and no known cause that they fear us."

Some of this sounded familiar to me, and I realised he was taking passages from the Declaration of the Rights of Hybrids, which Johnny had written. How dare he do that!

Maman stood up to deliver her bit: "If they poured all the resources they're putting into the Gene Police and the Zone into finding a cure, they could find one in a couple of months, believe me. We know why they don't do it. That's why we have to fight them!"

The lecture turned into a list of assignments for the day. A detail started on the washing up. The rest prepared to head into a warehouse for drill practice. Children.

I pushed my way through and caught up with Maman. "How old is he?" I hissed.

"What?" she said.

"Thom — your boyfriend. How old is he?"

"Eighteen," she admitted.

"But he's horrible! And he could be your son — my brother!"

She looked helpless. "He needs me," she said eventually. "How can he do this on his own? Look, someone has to take care of these children!"

"Pah!" I spat and ran away from her. Right then I hated Gunn. But I hated her more. I realised how Papa must have felt. I'd been right at the start. It was a trap here. I could no more leave than could any of the other Greys. Outside, I wouldn't last ten minutes before being picked up. I had to find a way to calm down. I had to find a way to turn this around. I had to wait.

The days passed in exercises and lessons. Gunn told us everything he knew about military history, campaigns, guerrilla warfare. We would spend hours practising karate and weight training to get fit – except the son of the owner, who was somehow excused. They had few weapons. But a small select group, I soon found out, did have work making explosives – compounds, timing devices, detonators, triggers – in a separate space, under the supervision of a hybrid the same age as Gunn called Stiletto. He had long black hair, a stupidly shaped beard and sideburns, and always wore black. It was impossible to tell his nationality. This guy was no charmer. He took an instant dislike to me and I could only watch at a distance as he showed a group of four how to mix explosive compounds from common ingredients and pack them in different containers for different effects. They said that the explosives would only be used to create a disturbance, never to kill or hurt anybody. How could they be sure, I wondered?

I found out a few days later. Gunn, Stiletto and a couple of others were going out on a mission. It was the day of the deadline for hybrids to report to the Gene Police and enter the Zone. We watched it on TV. A long queue of ambulances and Gene Police wagons led to the security gates around the sealed entrances to the estate. Cameras weren't allowed inside, but the BBC had a helicopter flying overhead that showed more queues of hybrids being processed and milling around aimlessly. But most of what went on was hidden inside the twentieth-century concrete warren. I thought of Cheri and everyone else from Salvation House, trying to imagine what it was like for them.

"Aren't you glad you're not in there, *ma chérie?*" asked Maman.

"Yes, but so what? I don't want to be here either," I confessed. "I want to be free. I want my old life back."

"Don't we all? But that's all gone now. This is the new world. But is it going to belong to the Gene Police or to us? That's why we have no choice but to fight."

She explained that the team had gone out to create a disturbance that would mark the day and demonstrate that we would not tolerate being treated like cattle. Sure enough, as we continued to watch, television news began to filter through about explosions in three places across the city – all outside Gene Police headquarters which had been left relatively unguarded. All the bombs had been set to detonate at the same time. Warnings had been telephoned through to allow time to evacuate the areas, so casualties were avoided. The incendiaries did little damage – just started small fires.

I had to admit it was exciting, watching this happen and knowing we'd caused it. Knowing that as the pundits were all asking questions about who was behind it and what did it mean, we alone knew the answers.

Then I gasped to see Gunn's face appear on the screen. Dressed in battle fatigues, he addressed the camera in a pre-recorded statement to explain why the action had taken place. "Actions like these will continue until all hybrids are released and taken into proper care," he intoned. "And we want to see billions of pounds put into finding a cure using public money without any secret patents, so that no companies can make a profit out of it. It should be done for the common good."

I watched Maman watching him and saw the look of pride on her face.

"Somebody hand delivered a DVD this morning," she explained.

The team arrived back, high on their success, to a rapturous welcome. I looked away while Gunn and Maman embraced happily.

I decided it was time to make my move. I went straight up to Gunn. "That was brilliant what you just did. I didn't know you could do stuff like that." I hoped my lie was convincing.

"Thanks, Kes," he smiled. "I knew you'd come round to our way of thinking sooner or later."

"But you know what would be even more brilliant?" I asked innocently. "What about attacking the Centre for Genetic Rehabilitation and letting everybody out? Or at least rescuing my friend Johnny. You know, the one who wrote the Declaration of the Rights of Hybrids? He's a prisoner in there. I think he would be a great addition to your team, don't you? Why not do it now, while everybody's attention is on the Quarantine Zone?"

He looked at me and began to crack one of his wolfish smiles. "Your mate wrote that? Hey, you know, that's not such a bad idea, Kes!"

19. Love

Yet another day, another grey, smelly, rubbish-strewn day at the dump. There had been several deliveries, but two of them had been bulldozed straight into the ground without giving us any chance to scavenge. Slash and I were concealed, waiting for the vehicles to depart so we could head down and see what the day's pickings would bring. They finally left around five o'clock and we were just about to scramble down when a lorry entered the grounds I hadn't seen before. It bore the logo of Richardson's Recycling.

I held Slash back and we watched as it halted, and out stepped a beautiful girl with a halo of black hair and a man carrying a rifle. They looked like they weren't here to work. I turned up my camera's digital zoom. Now I could tell the man was a hybrid. The rifle was part of his arm.

What about the girl? She had her hand in her pocket. As I watched she took it out – it was a mobile phone. I turned to Slash. "They're hybrids. It's cool, p'raps they're looking for someone they know, one of us. Let's go down."

"I don't recognise them myself," he said and we ran down the slope kicking rubbish as we went. As we got near, the girl gave a cry of recognition.

She flung her good hand up to her face and started running towards us – it was me she was looking at. Next thing she was flinging her arms around me and crying on my filthy T-shirt. I didn't know what the hell was going on.

I guessed I should know her, but I couldn't find a trace in my memory. Unless – those people who brought me here had mentioned a girl with black hair. Her arms encircled my torso, her hand and phone met in the small of my back. My own hands hung by my side. I guessed I must have known her well. I felt stupid.

Slowly, experimentally, I brought my arms up underneath hers and round her shoulders. She relaxed, but I still felt awkward. My arms seemed to recognise what they held. Had they done this before? In what circumstances? I inhaled her perfume, this wonderful scent drifting into a sensor under my chin, and suddenly something clicked inside. I don't know what the smell reminded me of, but there came a vision of sunshine, long hair, smiling eyes and laughter. Where did that come from? Kestrella – oh yes, that was her name – felt the change inside me and pressed against my shoulder blades. I began to sob. I had no choice.

Yes, it is possible to cry without eyes: my body heaved, my chest expanded and collapsed rapidly. Strange noises emitted from my speakers. I had no idea what was appearing on my screen. All that time with the Flotsam, I'd given no thought to that. Now I began to panic. I shouldn't let myself go like this. I'd seen what had happened to some of the others when they'd given in to their emotions. Self-pity gave way to self-abuse, like attacking the inorganic parts of their bodies, smashing their electronic attachments. I'd seen a girl like Kestrella punching concrete with her mobile phone. Later, she was weeping from the pain, fragments of metal, wires and skin hanging off her arm. She couldn't talk properly, couldn't think. Then the fever came. With some people, it left after a while. But with her, secondary infections set in. A week later, she was dead. Maybe it was what she'd wanted. For me it was another reason for keeping the floodgates closed.

I pushed Kestrella away. I couldn't see properly. I remembered about a certain block of ice, that precious block of ice in my heart. I could feel it beginning to melt. I was aware that Kestrella had sat down beside me. She took my hand, she was whispering. What was she saying?

"It's OK, it's OK to cry, it's good. You'll feel better. Don't fight it."

I tried to speak but I couldn't put words together. Exactly what I'd feared. Now she was stroking the back of my head.

"You need to cry. You've been through hell, Johnny."

Suddenly the sobs came back. For no reason, no reason at all. I began to hit the side of my screen with the palm of my hand. She grabbed hold of my hand to stop me damaging myself. I resisted at first. Slowly, awareness of my surroundings returned, and there she was kneeling in front of me, gazing up with concern. Why was she doing this? I felt the block of ice melting inside, I felt the ground open up beneath me. Then I saw her hand on my wrist and looked for her other hand, the one that was a mobile phone. I saw how inflamed it was – bright red and flaking.

"Look – look at your wrist!" I managed to say.

"Yes, I know. It's flared up since I last saw you. That damn I-So-L8. No good any more." She hid her hand away.

"Does it hurt?"

"It's OK," she managed. "Compared to you it's nothing."

Meanwhile, the rifle hybrid had been talking with Slash. Slash had explained about the Flotsam, what they did, how they survived. How they thought they would all probably die here, as some of them already had. They were buried with the other rubbish.

"How many of you are there?" he asked.

"Thirty," Slash said. "At the last count."

The rifle man looked as though he were working something out in his head. Then he spoke. "I'm going to make you an offer. All of you. You like living here?"

"Sure, it's like the Paris Hilton," Slash replied, looking at me.

"How would you like it?" I said.

"And you all're hybrids?"

"Sure. All types."

"So," he said. "How about if I said you can all come back with us and join our organised group of hybrids fighting for our rights, fighting the Gene Police? In exchange for a roof over your heads, a square meal once a day, security and friends, you would be joining the Hybrid Resistance Army, led by yours truly, Thom Gunn."

We stared at him.

"You know," Kestrella told me. "They're all inspired by that thing you wrote, Johnny – I mean – no, I'm sorry, I can't call you Pixelface. You remember – the Declaration of the Rights of Hybrids."

"The what?"

Gunn said, "Yeah, Kestrella said you wrote that. I wanna say that I'm so proud to meet you, Johnny, or Pixelface, or whatever you call yourself." He held out his hand. I took it limply. "That – manifesto – is what inspired us to start the HRA."

"I don't remember anything about it," I said.

"Well, I do," said Slash. "I read it once. I thought, all right. That's the business. That guy rocks. It speaks for all of us. Hey, I never knew you wrote that! You kept quiet about it!"

But search as I might I could find no trace of it in my files, whatever it was. "I'm sorry…" I muttered.

Gunn took my arm. "Come with us. You've had a hard time, comrade. We'll tell you all about it when we get to HQ. What about the rest of them, Slash? Will they want to come?"

"He's our leader, Thom," said Slash. "If Pixelface says we go, what's to stay for?" He looked at me expectantly. Kestrella's expression made me go weak at the knees.

I shrugged. "Can't be any worse than here, can it?"

Two hours later, all thirty of us were crammed into the back of the lorry, with Gunn, Kestrella and myself in front. Kestrella held my hand as she recounted how they found me.

"I thought you were still in the CGR. I wanted Thom to rescue you. He had contacts in the peace camp, so he called his friend and she said the army had evicted them from the land a couple of days earlier. They're now banned from going within ten miles of the place. But then she said they'd found you – that somehow you'd managed to escape – and she told us where they'd brought you. So that's how we got here! Oh, I'm so happy I found you!"

I told her what I'd pieced together: something about a combined retro and software virus they'd given me to wipe my memory clean. But I didn't know how I'd escaped – it was all a blank. Kestrella said she'd help me get my memory back when we got to their hideout.

"I'm not sure I want it back," I replied.

"Don't talk like that," she responded. "You've got to know who you are. You've got to face the truth. What would your friend Bruce Lee say?"

"Bruce Lee? Who's he?" I said. "Somebody I know?"

"Oh, Johnny! You've got so much catching up to do. They must have really damaged you."

The lorry rolled on. When we were safe inside the scrapyard, Gunn took the rest of the Flotsam to meet the resident members of his Hybrid Resistance Army. Together with those living off-site, there would now be nearly a hundred of them, he said, and you could see his eyes gleam with the thought of it. But he looked at me kind of suspiciously, as if I was a potential threat to his power.

Kestrella showed me the shower. Underneath the hot water I scrubbed off the accumulated grime and dust of the last few weeks from my skin, my hair, my fingernails, my plastic. It was luxury.

Afterwards I felt much better. She was waiting for me as I emerged from the bathroom wearing a white towelling bathrobe that Gunn had lent me.

"Mmm, you smell clean and bright as a newborn lamb," she said.

I let my pixels form a rainbow. The rainbow glittered and sparkled and turned upside down into a radiant smile.

"You don't really know who I am and probably I don't really know who you are, but right now I don't care," I heard her say. "I just want you to know that I haven't been able to get you out of my mind all the time we've been apart. I think you are the most amazing boy

I have ever met: talented, thoughtful, kind… Come to me, come here," she whispered.

I didn't recognise myself in her description, but I approached gingerly. She held out her arms and slowly, warily, I moved into them. My chin resting upon her shoulder, our ears pressed against each other's, flesh against flesh. We sank into each other like feet into quicksand.

"Tighter," she said. "I thought I'd never see you again, and never be able to tell you how I felt about you."

I felt the muscles in my body uncoil and a long groan fell out of my muffled speakers. We stayed like that for a while, feeling the warmth of each other's bodies, me savouring her delicious, flowery fragrance, the fingers of my left hand stroking her long hair, while hers combed the dampness of my locks.

At this point an older woman entered.

"Oh, Maman," said Kestrella. We drew apart a little and I recognised a family resemblance. "This is Johnny, the boy who was helping me look for you. Johnny, this is my mother, Jacquelyn. I found her – but I guess you don't remember she was lost!"

I didn't. Jacquelyn came over and placed a hand on each of our shoulders. She recoiled slightly at my appearance.

In my cracked electronic voice I said, "I don't know how to thank you for rescuing us."

Jacquelyn smiled, stiffly. "You don't have to say anything and you certainly don't have to thank us. We had to track you down in order to preserve my daughter's peace of mind! Really, we were getting so bored with her going on about you!"

Question marks flashed over my liquid crystals. "I don't know who you are," I said. "I'm sorry, it's what they've done to me."

"You've been through a terrible experience," Kestrella said. "But it's over now. You're with friends."

"I didn't know I had any," I said.

"Oh, my precious, I'm your friend! And now we're together I'm never going to leave you again. Listen," she said. "I have an idea for how you can get your memory back. Come here!" She took me by the hand and led me into an office in the corner of the warehouse where there was a computer connected to the Internet. Her mother watched us leave with an expression that left no doubt she was disturbed by her daughter's choice of boyfriend.

"Once," said Kestrella, "you told me that you backed up your files all over the Internet, splitting them and putting them in different places, encrypting them or something. I don't know. Anyway, why don't you have a look? Here, I'll sit by you while you do it."

And so I did. I used the Internet connection to explore. At first, I wasn't sure what I was doing. But somewhere in my files I'd already found server addresses, usernames and passwords, and I'd wondered why they were there. By typing in some of these randomly and getting results Pixelface was able to realise how Johnny had organised and hidden his work.

Kestrella sat behind me with her arms draped over my shoulders. Every so often I'd utter little grunts of satisfaction, or shouts of frustration. Finally, hours later, I logged out and turned around gently to find that she'd gone to sleep, her cheek against my back. I felt like a different person. I lifted her shoulders and she raised her eyelids.

"It's coming back. There's still big gaps – it's like a jigsaw with pieces missing. For example, I found my blog site with the Declaration on it. And I've discovered who you are. You came into my life and rescued me from the streets." Her hand was exploring my hands. I tried, by brushing my fingers tenderly over hers, to say how I felt in a way that seemed more human than my voice could.

"Yes," she smiled. "I did. And now I've rescued you again. Seems to be becoming a habit. Do you know why I did it this time?"

I shook my head. And I heard her say words I thought I would never hear from anybody. "Because I think I love you, Johnny."

I had no idea how to respond to this. To start with, she used the name Johnny. But from my limited new knowledge I didn't like the person that Johnny was. He was bitter and full of hate and anger. Before that I'd just read that I was Robert – the name my mother had given me. But I knew next to nothing about him either because I'd written little about that. More recently, I'd been Pixelface. I guessed I felt more like him than any of them. But he was quickly fading. The one thing I did know was that life was changing around me faster than a security software upgrade and I was changing to keep up with it, as well as changing within my body. I was very aware that Creep was gradually taking over my body, modifying my cells. Would my self-knowledge ever be able to keep up with all these changes?

For now, I decided not to worry about any of this and just enjoy the moment. We hugged for a time without measure and then I said: "Here's something funny. I just found it in one of my files. Shortly after I met you I wrote that I could never have a girlfriend because no girl'd ever want to go out with someone she couldn't kiss."

"Oh!" Kestrella laughed and started pecking my neck with rapid kisses. "Any girl with any sense would love you for what they can see inside and not care what you look like! It's like me thinking nobody would want to go out with me because they can't hold my hand."

"That's really stupid," I blurted. "I mean, there's lots of other things to hold!"

And we both burst out laughing. My pixels painted a desert island all sunshine, sand, blue sea and palm trees.

"Yes, it is like paradise, isn't it?" she said. "God, Johnny, you were so closed up. You were so 'I can do it on my own, sod off'. Like you really had something to prove."

"Yes, but I couldn't know that till I'd lost everything. Now I'm starting again from scratch. I feel – like a new man!"

"You are!" she laughed. "In more ways than one."

We ate with the others – takeaways donated by Charlie Richardson, the yard's owner. Slash sat by me – like the other Flotsams he was happy. I'd never seen them happy.

"I always thought you'd get us out of that dump, Pixelface," he smiled. "You're a hero, man!" It felt good, but it didn't seem to me like I'd done anything.

"Yeah, man – decent nosh! Forgotten what it tasted like!" shouted Metal Gristle further down the table, waving his spoon in the air. I looked at the people I'd come to think of as my friends – Wirey, Plasma, Remote, Poker and the rest. They were all tucking in like they hadn't eaten for months. Well, they hadn't, not properly that is.

"I guess that means you want to stay," I said.

"You know what they say," joked Gunn. "An army marches on its stomach! Of course you're going to stay – and give the Gene Police a taste of their own medicine! Eh, Johnny?" He turned to look seriously at me, and the rest of the Flotsam looked too, waiting for my reaction. But I wasn't convinced yet.

"I need to know more about what you're up to first, Thom," I replied.

So later, I looked in on the training. In a cleared space inside a warehouse, seventy youngsters were doing a ramshackle drill. Somehow, I didn't feel like joining in. Something about it didn't feel right. A bunch of underage misfits thinking they could take on the state, led by an elder boy with a rifle for an arm. Kestrella sniffed and said she wouldn't trust Thom Gunn further than she could throw a tissue. Followed by Gunn's suspicious gaze she led me back to the office, where I continued my research. I was following obscured data trails through the net to collect pieces of the jigsaw that was me, trying to fit them together without a guide. Pretty soon I came across something that made me shout out loud.

"What is it?" asked Kes.

"I've found a mailbox. Five weeks' unanswered mail: 5000 messages."

"Uh-oh. Nightmare. Maybe I'll go and work out for a bit while you sort through them. *Au revoir!*"

She kissed my head and left. I began to trawl through it, sorting out the spam, hate mail and mail from online buddies. Pretty soon I noticed 30 emails from the same .gsi.gov.uk email address – that's a government address. Curious. Why would somebody in the government be trying so hard to get in touch with me?

I opened one and got another big surprise. I printed it and went off to show Kestrella.

"It's from my dad," I said. "He wants to meet me."

20. Deserters

After the following morning's breakfast and morale-boosting speech from Gunn, we were about to leave the mess room for the office again while the others dispersed for their duties, when Gunn approached Johnny. He put his hand on Johnny's shoulder and gave him a shot of his wolfish grin.

"Well? What do you think, mate? You've seen our little operation. You know, your experience and skills could be very useful to us. I hope you decide to stick around."

Maman had come up to his side and he draped his arm around her shoulder. No matter how many times I saw this it still made me feel icky inside.

"I do hope you say yes," she said. "After all, with us you have friends – we'll look after you."

"Sure will," chipped in Gunn. "That's what an army's about – comradeship, support, solidarity." He bent forwards to Johnny's ear. "Come and see me later," I heard him whisper. "I'll let you in on some of our plans. I'd be interested in your opinion."

Gunn and Maman walked away holding hands, to begin the task of conducting the day's training and planning sessions.

"God, I can't stand it," I hissed to Johnny. "They're getting worse. Thom is so cocky, he thinks he's really scored with Maman. The former famous cover model. I've no idea why she's doing this."

Johnny nodded. "Yeah, but see it from her point of view. He represents her best chance of survival. She's just swapped one alpha male for another."

"Yeah, but why does she need one at all?" I said.

When there was a break, we went to where Gunn and Maman were working together above the mess room, in a mezzanine area at the back of the warehouse. Gunn was pleased to see us.

"Good to see you two. How's the memory reconstruction going? I've been meaning to ask you, Johnny, what was it like in the CGR?"

I sat next to Johnny while he related what he'd managed to piece together from the remaining few scraps of a diary he'd kept while in the CGR that he had been able to retrieve. He left out the bit about meeting his mother, which he'd told me before. Gunn was interested in the tests, and the way that the inmates were kept separated from each other.

He asked about the security systems, but Johnny was only able to produce a few details. He mentioned a prisoner kept in an isolated building. This really got Gunn excited. "Weren't you able to find out who he was, not even a clue?"

"I think he – or she – was inside a caged building under separate guard. I can't remember if anyone I spoke to had anything to do with them."

Maman and Gunn turned to each other. "Whoever it is must be important, or dangerous," said Gunn with a special light in his eyes.

"And they must be really scared of him or her to separate them like that," agreed Maman. "Do you think the wire mesh means something?"

"It could be to prevent communication with the outside world, by radio waves or microwave. Perhaps they have a form of comms rewrite…"

"We've got to find out who it is," said Maman.

"Yes, we could use ability like that. It's not going to be easy to try and get everybody out of the Zone."

While they were getting excited, I nuzzled up to Johnny. My whole body tingled with a different sort of electricity as our hands touched and part of my mind began to wonder if we could communicate with each other on a data transfer level this way. I could see Maman glancing with distaste at my behaviour.

Touché, I thought. We walked off together to the office.

"Come on, let's think about what you're going to do about this invitation from your dad," I said.

"Yes. It could be a trap," said Johnny. "He is a government man. But I've got to find out more about myself. There's still big gaps in my knowledge. You've no idea what it's like reaching for memories and finding chunks of blankness. Some of it could be really important. So maybe I should see him."

"How did he find your email address anyway?"

"They could easily have stolen it from my system while I was in the CGR," he said. "I'm going to email him and find out more. I'll set up a new account just for that purpose to protect myself. No harm in that, is there?"

I wasn't sure. But that's what he did, and an answer came promptly back.

>

>

>

Dear Robert,

I can assure you there is no subterfuge in my desire to see you. You will at all times be free to leave. But I do so want to meet the son I have missed for two years. I didn't even know if you were still alive. There is much I have to tell you, which I think will be of great interest...

With very best wishes,
Your father, David

"He sure writes funny," I said. "So formal."

"Yeah," said Johnny. "Stiff as a board."

"Well?" I said.

"I have to see him," he said. "Or I will forever wonder what it was about."

There followed a flurry of emails while arrangements were made. We would meet the following day at his father's house.

"Shouldn't you meet somewhere neutral?" I asked.

"There is nowhere neutral," Johnny said, "if you think about it. The security forces can go anywhere and monitor anywhere they want to. For all we know they are monitoring us now. So if he chooses his own house to meet at, he must have a reason."

"We'll have to tell Thom and Maman," I said.

We returned to that mezzanine level where Gunn and Maman were plotting. All the other kids were elsewhere in a training session being run by one of the older hybrids. When Johnny told him what he wanted to do, Gunn shifted uneasily in his chair, nervously drumming his rifle against the desk.

"Don't like it," he said. "For all we know they'll capture you, drain your memory banks and find out all about us."

"But I have to go," Johnny said. "Surely you can understand?"

"Bad attitude, kid," said Gunn. "The HRA saved your life and we're the only hope left for hybrids, far as I'm aware. I can't have us put at risk like that."

"But you can't stop us going!" I said.

"Johnny, this is not just about you," Gunn said. "It's about all of us. You better learn to accept orders. Find another way to get your memory back."

"Orders?" said Johnny. "I don't recall having agreed to join your army."

"There's a war on, boy," said Gunn. "It's us or them. And if you're not on their side you must be on ours, whether you like it or not. Ergo, you're a soldier now. Besides, we took our inspiration from what you wrote

– the Declaration. 'Hybrids must unite' – remember that?"

"I do remember now. But this kind of outfit is not what I had in mind." Johnny took my hand. "Come on, let's go."

As we were descending the steps I heard Maman murmur in Gunn's ear, thinking I couldn't hear: "Thom, why not let him go, but keep Kes here. She is only fifteen."

I turned back. "Maman! That's not fair!"

"But I want you here with me, darling."

"You're only saying that because you don't like Johnny!" I shouted. "But how do you think I feel about him?" I pointed at Gunn.

Gunn moved quickly to defuse the situation. "Hey, hey, let's change the subject."

"Yes, yes, what a good idea," agreed Maman hurriedly.

"Look what we're doing, Johnny. As you wrote, 'If the government does not protect us, then hybrids have no choice but to defend themselves, by any means at their disposal'. That's what we're doing. See this map? The location of every Gene Police station in London. Here's the Quarantine Zone. And here is the CGR. Now soon they plan to close down the CGR and move its operations into the Zone. All hybrids and those who work with them will be in there. Here's the route from the CGR to the Zone. We reckon, as they come here, through Bermondsey, that we can ambush a convoy. Pick them off, guerrilla style. We will try to target the special prisoner you told us about. What do you think?"

Johnny thought. "You really want to know what I think?" he said. "You're living in a dreamworld."

"You what?" said Gunn with genuine confusion. Some of the kids had started wandering into the mess room below. They looked up when they heard us.

Johnny sighed. "Don't you realise what you're up against? You seem to think this is like some comic book adventure and you're superheroes. Instead, it's just a bunch of sad, scared and dangerous people running around and smashing into each other, causing damage cos they didn't think through the consequences of what they were doing. It's all random."

I found myself nodding in agreement.

"No," said Maman. "What we want is a better world. They're just selfish."

"I bet that's what they believe too," I said to her.

"Who was it once talked about the selfish gene?" continued Johnny. "Have you thought about that? It's our genes inside us making us look out for our best interests, trying to get passed on to the next generation. You and the government are just pawns of your genes acting out roles they've decided for you. Well, I am fed up with it all. I don't want to be anybody's pawn."

"You should side with your friends, with those whose interests you share," added Maman. "Of all people you should know that."

"You mean this ragged army?" said Johnny, and there was a gasp from those below who were listening. I grabbed his hand, but he didn't seem to notice. "Sure I believe in solidarity, but you don't stand a chance against the Gene Police, the army and the SAS once they get wind of you. Besides, who makes all the decisions round here? This hardly seems to be an example of democracy and co-operation – just a one man show!"

The whole room was silent and watching. "Thom." It was Maman's turn to step between us and Gunn and whisper to him. "It's clear we have to let them go. Both of them."

"But an army relies on discipline, on order," Gunn hissed. "If we don't have discipline, we're lost. That's what my dad taught me. We have to make an example of them."

"Yes, but suppose we say we're giving them compassionate leave?" she whispered.

Gunn relaxed a little and looked down at all the pairs of eyes waiting to see what he would do. "All right," he relented and turned to Johnny. "We can't stop you going to meet your dad. But in return you must help us. You must try to find out more about that prisoner. You must find a way to tell us."

"OK, I'll try," said Johnny, realising it was the only way we would be let out.

"And take every precaution to protect your memories of here. I dunno – delete them, encrypt them, whatever."

"I promise."

"And don't expect me ever to come and rescue you again. I've got all these other soldiers to take care of. And we have a war to prepare for!" And he turned back to all those faces which gazed up in admiration. I felt kind of sick.

Johnny and I went down and left the warehouse. Nobody stopped us, not even the former Flotsam.

The next morning we gathered what few possessions we had and were ready to go. Johnny took my hand in his. "You don't have to come with me, you know," he said.

I glared at him with a look that would melt lead. "I know. But now I've found you again, I'm never going to let you out of my sight. We're together to the end, OK?"

His body was shaking with emotion. "Yes. To the end. I promise. The only thing is—"

"What?" I asked suddenly afraid.

"Nothing," he said.

I went to say goodbye to Maman. We hugged, knowing it was possible we might never see each other again, but afraid to say so.

"You have to go, don't you," she said.

I nodded. "And you have to stay."

She nodded.

"Take care, OK?" I said.

"*Bien sûr. Et toi*," said she, a tear in her eye. "*Je t'aime. Adieu, ma chérie.*"

Johnny said goodbye to Slash, Metal Gristle and the other Flotsam, who wished us good luck.

Slash said: "You'll be back, right?"

"Sure," said Johnny.

"Well, good luck – we're behind you, Pixelface. And take care. The Gene Police have eyes everywhere."

Johnny then took my hand and led me through the door to the outside world, the world of Keep Britain Normal.

Soon we were in an electric taxi purring across London. Maman had given us the number of a minicab firm whose owner was sympathetic to hybrids. We hid on the floor behind the seat so no one outside would see us, unable to avoid the endless patter of the middle-aged driver.

"You wouldn't believe how bad it's got. No end of taxi firms gone down the tube. Everybody afraid to go out, see? Nobody's got any dosh anyway what with the crash an' all. An' as for the tourist trade, bottom's fallen so far out of the market it's at the bottom of the Atlantic. America, land of the brave? Don't make me laugh. Nobody's seen a Yank for ten month round 'ere. They're all scared they'll catch summat nasty, an' you know what that means! As if any tourist has picked anything up from a dirty weekend in Soho apart from the clap."

"What about you?" I asked. "Aren't you afraid yourself — you might get the auto rewrite?"

"Look, girlie, if I'm gonna pick anything up, I'll pick it up no matter what I do. I been drivin' a cab for twenty year an' it's never done me no 'arm. Natcherly we take precautions — we change the cab every quarter so I don't get too close to one model. Costs a bob or two but — D'ya hear about Pete of Camberwell Motors? Shockin'. 'E came down with it — only passed 'is test six months. His ma wouldn't even let him in the garage. Lived in a lock-up in Norwood till someone shopped him and them Gene Police tossers came and towed 'im to Peckham."

I contemplated the life of Pete, cowering in the dark in a smelly lock-up garage in South London, relying on his friends to bring him food, oil and water and dreading every set of approaching footfalls outside.

I turned to Johnny, my hand on his leg. He was miles away, perhaps surfing the net somewhere through the onboard system. Outside, London sped past. Traffic hadn't flowed this freely for sixty years. It was eerie. This was what fear did to city life.

"Missus has been goin' on at me to stop for months. I says to 'er, who's going to bring 'ome the bacon? She don't make enough dosh cleaning airports specially since 'ardly anyone comes 'ere any more. And me drugs bill – them Recombi-Norms and the like – cost nearly as much as the mortgage."

And that was money going straight into the bank account of Papa's company, I reflected.

"Mind you, one silver lining to all this – you don't 'ave to listen to people having loud, intimate conversations on their mobile phones any more, do yer? And the phut-phut-phut of their iPods."

He broke off into a wheezy laugh. I asked him what he thought was the cause of the pandemic.

"Bleedin' obvious, innit? It's the Chinese. Who makes all them gadgets we use? They've gone and put some bug into 'em so they can take over when we're all compost. They're just jealous, in't they?"

"Jealous? What of?" I said. This was a new one on me.

"Our country. Over there it's either too 'ot or too dry, not enough food, an' their coastal cities is all drownin'. When we're gone they'll colonise 'ere, see?"

I lapsed into silence. Everybody had a theory about where the virus came from. For some it was CIA labs in America: the Yanks wanted to destroy Europe as a commercial competitor. For others it was GM food or nanotechnology – bugs loosed into the environment that had started evolving and got out of control. Some said it was because we were too reliant on material goods and needed to get back to living on the land: the plague was nature's revenge against humanity. Then there were those who believed human beings were now redundant and this was another stage in evolution. And some religious nutters thought we were being punished by God for either a) worshipping material goods, b) our immoral lifestyle, or c) not praying often enough. Creep was the Devil's work.

I squeezed Johnny's hand. It felt so good to be with

him now. He turned to look at me.

"What's the matter?" he said.

"What do you mean?"

"You look worried."

"Yes, it's Maman. I was looking for her for so long and imagining all kinds of awful things had happened… even that she was dead. And when I found her…"

"…you discovered she'd gone simply because she wanted to," said Johnny, voicing my thoughts.

"Oh, how could she love that macho jerk?"

"Nearly there," announced the driver suddenly. "Twickenham."

We risked a peep through the window: a leafy avenue with massive houses hidden up long drives behind acres of wooded grounds.

"Bloody posh, isn't it? Wonder how he can afford to live here?" said Johnny.

"This isn't where you grew up?"

"Can't remember. Don't think so though."

The car lurched to the left throwing Johnny on to me. We took the opportunity to hug and he whispered, "I feel like a mouse walking into a lion's cage."

We paid off the cab and it scrunched away over the gravel. Hand in hand we turned to look at where it had left us. Night had almost fallen, and a few lamps lit the way through the gloom beneath arching beeches. We started walking.

"Even when I was at home, my dad was so distant we never connected. I wonder why he really wants to see me? I bet it's not to give me the keys to the family home."

"Whatever it is, we'll face it together," I said.

"Yes, but—"

"What?"

"Never mind."

"What is it, Johnny? There's something troubling you too, isn't there?"

"I'm not Johnny, Kestrella."

I was suddenly afraid. "What do you mean?"

"I mean I'm changing. How do you know I'm the person you think you love? I have no idea who I am, so how can you know?"

I breathed again. "I just do, silly. It doesn't matter what you call yourself, you're still the same sweet guy. It's how you behave that matters. Stop thinking so much!"

"I dunno. Thinking seems to be what I'm made to do. Anyway. Come on. We might as well go and see what my dad's like."

We rounded a bend in the drive to discover a large Georgian structure fronted by a portico flanked by a pair of stone lions. The main house had at least four storeys, including the attic, and there were a number of outbuildings.

Johnny let out a long whistle through his speaker. "Ah well, here goes nothing."

And he led me up the steps to knock on the front door.

21. Meet the Ancestors

I had Farah take the youngsters into the smoking room first. We could have an aperitif there prior to dinner. I studied them on the CCTV screen from the control room. They had no idea they were being watched as they ambled slowly among the huge leather chairs, examining the portraits on the walls. Good. That was just what I wanted. How romantic they looked, if a touch macabre to those unfamiliar with the disease.

He'd grown a lot: a good eight centimetres. Lanky, like his uncle on his mother's side.

Farah had told them I would be along shortly and brought them drinks. I was interested to watch how my son imbibed his. He had slightly refined the process since leaving us.

I studied the girl. She moved with assurance far from the awkwardness usual for that age, and this betrayed a certain maturity that matched her lovely appearance. Here was a girl commencing the peak of her attraction, glowing with sexual power, but not yet cynical and overly aware of her impact upon others. Even her affliction she bore with grace.

I sent a message to Farah, advising her to initiate sub-plan B. This involved a suggestion that they shower and change before I, now regrettably delayed, could attend. Separate showers were offered in the east annex, and a small wardrobe of clothes bought especially, following the advice of my informants on their respective sizes.

I took the opportunity to catch up with some reading of reports and preparation of material for the minister's red box. He does like to be kept informed.

But we all only know what we are told or trouble to find out for ourselves, don't we? And bothering to find out for themselves is usually far too much effort for most people.

It is not knowledge that is power, so much as the control of the gathering and supply of the same. My distant ancestor – another Robert – knew that to perfection.

When they re-emerged into the smoking room, they were in clothes of my choosing. The girl was resplendent in a casual suit of brushed cotton, of a shade matching her eyes, that accentuated the curve of her waist. Italian shoes, a silver necklace and earrings, and a coral clasp for her hair completed the picture. She seemed happy with the choice. Robert looked more uncomfortable in a pair of woollen trousers flecked in brown and orange, and a rye-green knitted shirt. His hair was blow-dried and tied back into a ponytail. A touch more presentable.

I had ordered their own clothes to be burnt. They wouldn't need them any more.

It was now that I made my entrance in my pewter-grey Singapore suit and a sky-blue silk shirt, with a tie bearing the family crest. I am not a tall man, but I nevertheless strive to create an impression.

I was introduced to Kestrella and gave myself the pleasure of kissing her dainty hand. I insisted that she know and henceforth vow to use Robert's true and given forename. I made small talk to put them at ease: the shooting and polo competition trophies in the cabinet, the African mementoes from the Boer War, the carved ivory elephants carrying sedan chairs given by the Rajah.

All the time awaiting the inevitable questions to which I had prepared my answers.

Finally they came and I said, "Why don't we wait until we dine? I do hope you are not averse to oysters, followed by a little venison in red wine?"

Mohamet had done a perfect job on the table. I enjoyed their reaction to the glittering, candlelit spectacle: awe, overlain by the suspicion that this was bait to lure them into the stickiest of webs. As, of course, it was, but there was little they could do about it now.

At the head of the dining room, above the mantelpiece, hung an enormous oil painting of our distant ancestor from the seventeenth century. He looked down with an expression of lofty disdain over his pointed beard upon the three of us, now seated at a table long enough for thirty.

Following a toast, which welcomed them to the house and wished the best for their future, Robert at last said: "But, Dad, is this really your house?"

"Indeed it is," I smiled.

"So who'd you steal it off?" he sneered.

I smiled. "Why, it is rightfully mine – and will no doubt be yours one day, if you are still here. I expect you are wondering why you were not raised here. The answer is simple: I had to wait to inherit it – from my uncle, who died childless. This is why we lived in exile in those awful suburbs among the great unwashed. Sometimes one just has to bide one's time until the appropriate moment comes to make one's move. Wouldn't you agree?"

"Suppose so," he replied, with all the articulacy of adolescence.

"Well, Robert, how have you been?" I enquired after the oysters had arrived. "Your mother says you have become a resourceful chap. You must have done, or you would not have the dubious distinction of being the first person ever to have absconded from the Centre for Genetic Rehabilitation."

"I did have a little help," he said, sipping the puréed oysters which I'd had the kitchen prepare especially.

"Nonsense!" I replied. "That is not what the official report says," and I winked at him. It took him a couple of beats for the old penny to drop.

"I... see," he said. "And what else does the official report say?"

"That you are dead," I said abruptly.

The old penny took a few more beats to descend a little further. I offered an encouraging smile.

"Um, er, you mean... they're not looking for me any more?"

"Not as such, no," I said cheerfully. "But that could always change."

I knew I should not underestimate the girl for she now said, "Er, why does the report say this?"

"Robert is my son." I gave another planned response. "Why should I not want to protect him from harm?"

Now he departed from the anticipated script with a violent outburst. "If that's true, why did you bloody well go and leave me? How could you do that?"

I must confess to being taken by surprise. "What do you mean?" I flustered slightly.

"Don't come all innocent with me! Don't play games with me!" He was shouting now, by increasing the volume of that odd mechanical voice of his. "You know what happened! I came back from school one day to find the house empty, you and Mum gone, and no trace of any of my own or anyone else's stuff in the house I'd spent all my life in – even if it did feel like a bloody mausoleum half the time! Where the hell did you go? Why did you abandon me like that? Why?"

I paused to regain my calm and waited for his storm to subside a little, popping another oyster into my mouth, then wiping my fingers and dabbing my lips with the monogrammed linen napkin before responding. "You mean you didn't see the note we left?"

His chair leapt back. "Note? Note? What bloody note?"

I could hardly contain my own incredulity. "The one we left on the kitchen table!"

"Kitchen table! I–I— What the hell do you mean?" he said.

"There was a letter for you. What did you do when you got home?"

"I–I can't remember!"

"Johnny – I mean, Robert – had his memory badly damaged in the CGR. He's only got some of it back," explained Kestrella.

"I see," was the best I could manage.

"You see what? Tell me what it said, Dad! Have I spent the last two years on the streets for nothing?"

I let Mohamet clear away the dishes before replying in as quiet a voice as I could manage. "You must realise the predicament your mother and I found ourselves in… following the onset of your… illness. Of course, as a child you took no interest in the positions we held in our public life, but, as you now know, your mother holds a senior medical management position in the battle against the disease, and I myself am the senior Civil Servant in the Home Office. That is to say, I have the honour of writing the official policy to combat the disease."

I was acutely aware of the intensity of the stares now upon me and what they signified, but I ignored them as Mohamet introduced the venison and accompanying dishes to the table. "Therefore, the discovery that our own offspring had become afflicted presented us with not only a personal tragedy but a tragic dilemma. Were we to declare the matter, you would have had to be put into the CGR, since our responsibilities were too great for us to care for you personally."

"But you're rich! You could have paid for this care!" Robert intervened.

"Now we are, yes. Or rather I am – your mother and I are now separated, but on reasonable speaking terms by the way."

"Oh, thanks for telling me," he chipped in again.

"But back then our circumstances were somewhat different. I wouldn't want to trouble you with the details but we were in substantial debt, and striving hard to pay it off. You must have noticed the lack of furniture and decoration. It was appalling – everything was in hock. Thankfully, my uncle's untimely death somewhat redeemed the situation – one's fortunes did an about-turn. But at the time, naturally, we did not want you in the CGR, knowing full well what fate would have awaited you. So you see, you could neither have become a Blue nor a Red. The only choice, then, was for you to become a Grey and seek your fortunes elsewhere."

"But the note! What did the note say?" said Kestrella.

"The note merely explained this situation and gave you certain detailed advice on what to expect, where to go for help, how to avoid the Gene Police and where you might find comrades and sanctuary, based on our intelligence advice from MI5."

I watched, this time with sadness, the old pennies drop further still, further than I had anticipated.

"Right," Robert said. "Sanctuary. Comrades. Help. Advice. All the things I had to do without for two years. I can't believe it."

I adopted silence for a moment, noticing that venison in red wine sauce had never lacked so much flavour. The others had not touched theirs (in Robert's case another purée). "I'm afraid so. When we didn't hear from you, we thought the worst. Or that you must hate us so much that you wanted to punish us with your silence."

"As, of course, I did."

"And your mother blamed me for forcing the wrong choice upon us and left me. But it was her decision as well, you know. Not just mine." I took a large gulp of wine to regain my composure. "Hm. In a way I imagine that congratulations are in order. You certainly hid yourself well. Our best intelligence failed to find you, or, when it did, you had already moved on. Until the happy accident when your trajectory happened to coincide with Malcolm Winter's cousin. And later that of the laughable Thomas Gunn."

"You know him?" asked Kestrella.

"Oh come, come, do you think us novices? We have a couple of moles in his little band. Now, please, do enjoy your meal. Perhaps, in time, you can come to forgive us, Robert. It's not our fault you didn't find the note."

"If only I could remember what happened – maybe I did find it. I just don't know. But if I had, why would I have been living the way I know I did?"

"Shall we just draw a line under this and move on?" I offered. "I do have some more interesting and positive news. But first, as you don't seem to have much of an appetite, why don't we withdraw to the drawing room?"

Mohamet took the signal and came to clear away the dishes and silverware as I guided them into the next room.

"I have a little present for you, Robert," I said after we had settled down with our coffee and, in my case, a glass of port. "Think of it as a kind of welcome back present."

I fished out a vellum envelope and handed it to him. Inside were two things: a cheque for £20,000 and a copy of our family tree. I smiled and stroked my upper lip with pleasure as I watched him examine them. "Is it not your birthday around now? You are sixteen soon; consider the cheque a birthday present."

He stared at it as if it were something from another planet.

"The family tree is to help you understand your heritage and birthright," I continued. "It is very much my fault, and I apologise for it, but while you were growing up this could not be revealed to you. The truth is, I had a fortune and lost it. At the gambling table. A fortune inherited from my father. Ah, not only that, but your mother's fortune too. I don't mind telling you that I felt absolutely awful. More than once I thought of topping the old self. But two things encouraged me to carry on: the knowledge that I could serve my country, as I still had an excellent position, and you, Robert."

I could see that he was enthralled by what he was reading. "Yes, you are part of one of the most illustrious families that has ever lived in this country. Members of the Cecil family have served in various high positions for thirteen generations and included Prime Ministers, Home Secretaries, and countless members of the aristocracy and Civil Service. All the portraits you have been looking at on the walls are of your ancestors."

It was true. The first noted nobleman in the line was William, for forty years chief secretary of state to

Elizabeth I, and the "chief architect of Elizabethan greatness" as I explained to Robert while pointing out his portrait above the fireplace. "And his son, your namesake Robert, was the first Earl of Salisbury, Queen Elizabeth's first minister and the kingmaker to James I. His picture you saw above the fireplace in the dining room. The line continues right up until Robert Gascoyne-Cecil, Viscount Cranborne, the last Tory leader of the House of Lords in the early twenty-first century."

It was then that I noticed what was on Robert's screen. Perhaps he was trying to tell me something, I don't know, but there was a face with its tongue hanging out. My voice faltered to a halt.

"Is there something you want to say, Robert?" I asked.

"Like, I am supposed to be impressed by all this?" he said.

"Impressed? I don't know, but don't you feel, well, lucky, to be part of such an illustrious family? I mean, it's not as if everybody can boast having so many important statesmen as ancestors."

Now his girl spoke up. "Why on earth should it make any difference who your ancestors were? It doesn't make you any more special than somebody whose mother was a prostitute or whose father was a tramp."

"No, of course not," I said quickly. "But it must surely change your perspective on things."

"Actually, Dad, it all looks the same when you see things from the gutter, which, by the way, is where I have been the last two years, if you remember."

"Yes, well, I assume that you are still in a state of shock due to your recent experiences," I said, trying to make excuses for him. "It must have been terrible for you, Robert. But – you've survived, you see, and that must say something about what kind of mettle you're made of, eh?" I tapped him gently on the left shoulder. Unfortunately, he flinched away.

"I suppose you're right," he said. "I really must try to develop a positive attitude. Thanks for the advice, Dad."

He lapsed into silence, slumping in a chair and taking his girlfriend's hand. I assumed they must be tired and suggested bed. I summoned Farah and asked her to take them to their rooms. They looked relieved. Poor things, they hadn't even brought any travelling bags with them. Even though they wouldn't be going back to where they came from.

Whether they liked it or not, this was going to be their home from now on.

22. The Tempting Offer

Subdued lighting softened the bedroom, with its linen sheets and a duvet the size of Trafalgar Square. An ensuite bathroom seemed to give endless hot water and the thick white towels were the size of sheets. A dressing gown was left out for me which I could live in. I was so exhausted that I just said goodnight to Kestrella, stumbled into my room and collapsed into a deep, inky slumber.

When I woke up, I don't know how much later, I lay in bed, half asleep, half awake, thinking. My father was clearly more bonkers than ever. Inheriting all this money had completely gone to his head, making him an upper-class twit. I had been beginning to get used to my fortunes sawing up and down like a yo-yo, but this was ridiculous.

I'd been able to find lots of files about Bruce Lee.... Apparently, we used to chat in my hours of need. Now he was standing by the dressing table and telling me not to worry.

"Hi, Johnny. Or whoever you are these days. Hardly recognise you in this place. Seems like you're on your uppers. But y'know, good luck and bad luck always follow one another, so I hope you're not thinking anything of it. Otherwise you won't be able to keep your cool while everyone around you is running about like headless chickens."

I got out of bed, trying to avoid seeing my reflection in a huge mirror that took up most of one wall.

"So, Bruce, what *are* you going to call me now?" I asked him as he appeared next to me. "I mean, who am I? Am I the little boy Robbie I thought I was when I was growing up? Or am I Johnny Online, the hybrid fugitive? What about Pixelface, the rubbish boy? Or what d'you think of Robert Cecil, aristocratic son of the Establishment? God, I'm confused."

"Who are you? That's easy," he winked, flicking a forefinger my way. "Just take a look in the mirror and you'll see…"

I glanced towards the full-length mirror. Cautiously, I took off my T-shirt and boxers and turned. I hated mirrors and reflections. It had been years since I'd examined myself. I knew I was a monster – ugly, scary and unnatural, a vision from healthy people's darkest fears or a figure of fun from a cheap science-fiction shoot-'em-up. But I forced myself to look. At first, I could only manage a sideways glimpse, out of the corner of my vision. A stick insect-like figure danced just out of sight, mocking me.

"Be brave, Johnny. It can't really hurt to know who you are," whispered Bruce.

I focused my camera further. The figure standing in front of me was tall and lanky with long gangly limbs in need of sunshine. The colour of his flesh varied from white to raw pink to grey to blue, like a map with no key. At times the grey or blue pierced the surface as what looked like plastic or aluminium surrounded by an eruption of rawness, pustules and yellow sores. I couldn't bear it and turned the camera away again.

"I know it's not pretty, Johnny. But it's something you got to do. Every man must know himself and dispel fear before he can stand proud and defeat his enemies. You want to know how I was able to punch and kick so hard? Because I didn't hold a single ounce of myself back. I gave every move 100 per cent. How could I do that? Only by conquering all fear and doubt. A mind divided is a mind that's weakened. I had to accept every part of myself – yes, you better believe there were parts of myself

I hated too. Everybody has them. Go on, take another good look. It won't be so bad as you think."

Reluctantly, I turned the camera on myself again. I wouldn't have done it if he hadn't told me to. I increased the digital zoom – it was easier to look at myself in detail. I could isolate the parts and pretend they weren't me. I saw my hair – shoulder-length and ginger – now at least I knew where that was inherited from. I moved closer and turned slightly so I could see where the screen came out of my head. It seemed to come from underneath the skin. It seemed to be joined to the skull itself, as if the bone somehow changed from the mineral calcium to polypropylene or whatever kind of plastic it was. Where it emerged, the edge was like the skin around a fingernail, but extremely flaky, flayed and infected. This, even though I put the I–So–L8 on it as often as possible. Kestrella was right – it wasn't working any more. Maybe the disease had become resistant.

I let the camera wander down my left arm. The discoloration continued underneath the surface, like veins, only they weren't veins. On the inside lower arm, wherever it surfaced, was the keyboard, only the keys were laid out irregularly, as if distorted by the biology. I scanned across my torso and the discoloration continued, but whatever was going on it never came to the surface anywhere else. If there were such things as a motherboard, a hard drive or processors, sound and video cards, or anything like that, they were hidden from view.

My speakers and microphone were under my chin. In the centre of my forehead, a small black dot – my photographic eye. I let it roam at will over my body. Gradually, I pulled back to examine the whole of my body from the top of my head to the tips of my toes. I began to sway and pose, hands on hips, like a model on the catwalk dancing to music. I pirouetted and danced to music in my head. Suddenly I found myself laughing. It looked so ridiculous. Weird, crazy, unconventional – but no longer quite so monstrous or scary.

"What did I tell you?" It was Bruce again. "Not so bad now, is it? Thing is, nothing is ever as bad as you think it's going to be. It's amazing what human beings can survive. I hope that's gone some way to answering your question. I think you can go out and face the world now." And he disappeared to wherever it is he goes when he's not there.

Turning to the wardrobe I found several sets of new clothes for me, most of which I wouldn't be seen dead in. I brushed my hair and put on jeans and a sweatshirt that didn't make me look like a total dork and finally wandered downstairs.

In the dining room, Kestrella was already up and looking gorgeous in a red kimono. I went up and put my arm around her. She did the same to me and kissed me on my left ear. I shivered; it tickled.

"You look great," she told me.

"Nobody ever told me that before," I said. "Do you really mean it?"

This time she kissed my right ear. "How dare you think I would lie to you!"

"And you look like a dream!" I whispered as best I could.

"Thank you," she said. "I have been told that before — but coming from you it sounds so much better."

"Sleep well?"

"Better than a long time," she said.

We hugged for while. In a funny way, I did feel like someone completely different, as if I had been strangely reborn. Someone stronger, someone just a little less frightened than a few days earlier. Was it really only a few days since I was living at the dump? It seemed like weeks. We began to graze on the breakfast left for us: fruit salad, muesli, yoghurt, jam, toast, ham, cereals and fruit juice. There were even specially liquidised versions for me.

"You know, your dad said that you kind of don't exist any more, didn't he?"

"Yeah. I always wanted not to exist and wondered what it was like. I didn't think it would be like this!"

We both burst out laughing.

"And all that cash your dad gave you…"

"Bad conscience money – or a bribe. It's bound to have strings attached," I said. "You wait and see."

After a while, Farah entered and announced that my father was waiting for us in his study. We followed her along a passageway, up some stairs and along another passageway to an oak-panelled door.

We found him dressed in an archaic tweed suit standing with his back to the big bay window, legs apart and hands clasped behind his back. After some meaningless pleasantries we sat around his desk. It was almost like a job interview. Perhaps, in his mind, it was.

"You know, this is where your great-great-great-grandfather used to come sometimes when he was in London," he began. "He was Prime Minister at a time when the British Empire embraced half the countries in the world. I like to imagine him cogitating on crucial state matters at this very desk. His strategic thought processes must have encompassed the entire globe. In those days much of the world was still unknown. He was one of the first people to use the new technologies –

electricity and the telephone – in his home. It scared the living daylights out of his guests!" He chuckled.

Kestrella looked at her mobile and sympathised with them.

"In many ways, I don't feel I'm so different from him," he said modestly. "I make recommendations which the minister acts upon. And, as you are both painfully aware, we face a time of unprecedented change and danger, affecting the future of the entire world."

Kestrella and I exchanged glances. We both wondered where this was leading.

"The plague is one of those events in the history of humanity that divides that history between before and after. Like before the Roman Empire, before Christ, before the atom bomb, or before the destruction of the Twin Towers. Perhaps it is even more important than any of those. And how we choose to respond to it will define the future of the human race. I can't think of anything more important. Can you?"

He looked deadly serious. We shook our heads, but said nothing.

"Tell me, if you had to protect the genetic health of the majority of this country, what would you do, Robert?"

I felt put on the spot. "I know one thing. I wouldn't resort to torture and imprisonment," I managed.

"Perhaps you wouldn't," he said. "I'm sure we don't intend that to happen. But nevertheless, time is of the essence, and sometimes to defeat a greater evil it is necessary to execute lesser ones. When you were in the Centre for Genetic Rehabilitation were you badly treated? Were you tortured or deprived of food? No, I don't think so. They were working on a way to cure you. They were working in the unknown. When you work in the unknown, beyond the fringes of science, the consequences cannot always be as benign as you would hope. There will always be an element of risk. Tell me honestly, Robert, do you think it could be otherwise?"

"But they left me in agony!" I cried.

He shrugged. "Sometimes the best medicine tastes awful…"

I couldn't think of a snappy reply. That didn't mean there wasn't one though.

"What do you think is the cause of the plague then?" I asked him. "Any idea?"

"We have the best minds working on it. We've examined all the theories – even the most crackpot. Yes, we know the one about Mu-Tech having dreamt it up in their labs. And the CIA and the Chinese and everyone else – including aliens from outer space! Then there are all the ideas about us having brought it on ourselves – genetic engineering, nanotechnology, implants, biochips… On balance, I think this is the most likely explanation. Something got loose, something got out of control. But even though we have a strong candidate, it doesn't mean we are a great deal closer to finding a cure. The virus is constantly mutating in response to its immediate environment. It can go through hundreds of generations in a day. It takes enormous computing power to keep up with that. So, as we don't have a cure, and as it's infecting more and more people, what's the sensible precaution to take, which has been taken by all epidemiologists in the past?"

This time it was Kestrella who spoke. "I know what you're trying to get us to say," she said. "That you're doing the right thing by containing all the hybrids in the Zone. But I don't believe it. I think you can be much more humane. You don't have to create a climate of fear – you can help people understand it."

"But we don't generate the fear!" he protested. "It's there already. If it wasn't for us there would be vigilantes on the streets hunting down hybrids and dealing out their idea of justice. Keeping the peace is what the Gene Police spend most of their time doing these days."

"So," I said, feeling that the conversation had gone on

long enough. "If we were to agree that the government's doing its best for us, what would happen to us?"

"Ah," he said. "That's good. I see you're thinking along the right lines. Well, then I would ask you both a question. And it would be this: would you join me and help me?"

"What?" we both said, stunned.

"If you choose to follow the example of your forebears and serve your country, you can live here in the lap of luxury for as long as you wish and be completely immune from the threat of going into the Centre for Genetic Rehabilitation or the Zone. What do you say?"

Kestrella and I stared at each other, speechless.

23. Pact with the Devil

"I'm kicking myself. You know how you can always think of a good retort afterwards?" said Johnny. "I should have said that no amount of what they're doing in the CGR 'for the greater good' justifies treating people like animals just cos they're ill. I really hate that phrase 'for the greater good'."

"He's trying to get you to agree to his policy. You, the author of the Declaration of the Rights of Hybrids. That would be a real coup for him, wouldn't it? I bet that's what he's trying to buy with his money and offer of a new life," I said, pretending to play with his fingers with my right hand. We were sitting on the bed in my bedroom. Actually, what I was doing was typing my response into his keyboard, and he was displaying his thoughts on his screen. This was because we'd agreed it was highly likely our bedrooms were bugged – perhaps even the whole house. For the same reason we kept his screen turned away from where we thought a camera might be concealed.

"He hasn't mentioned the Declaration yet. Hmmm. No network," said Johnny, who'd been scouring for a way on to the Internet. "He's got to have the Internet somewhere, but who knows what security systems the Home Office has dreamed up?"

I took the opportunity, seeing as I was using his arm, to run my fingers up his biceps. "No phones either. No one at the HRA has a mobile anyway, so we can't warn them that they've got a government mole. I wonder who it is? Oh, I hope Maman will be OK."

Johnny lay back on the bed and I gazed down at him, leaning on my elbow. "They're going to be busted, aren't they? He wants us to know that we can't go back there. We've got to be so careful. If we officially don't exist, and we're in his clutches – or under his protection, depending on which way you look at it – then anything could happen to us and nobody would know."

"Yes," I typed. "But let's look at it another way. He is your dad. And your mum helped you escape from the CGR. They're obviously still talking to each other. Maybe they really do want to make amends for how they treated you before…"

His screen went blank for a long time. Then it said: "We can't go back to the HRA if they're going to be busted, which seems more than likely. I'm not sure I like the idea of being singled out for special treatment though, just because I happen to be the son of a Civil Servant. I feel I ought to go to the Quarantine Zone with everyone else."

"Cheri will be there, and everyone from Sally House," I tapped.

"And I suppose they'll send the HRA there too." He went silent again, then said: "OK, how about this. Let's assume you're right. We could give him the benefit of the doubt for now and see what happens. I'm sure we can always find a way of getting picked up and taken to the Zone later if we want. But if we were to turn him down and go there now we'd never find out what he wants."

We returned down the wide staircase into the marble floored entrance hall, realised we were lost, retraced our steps, wandered along a corridor, down some other stairs and eventually found the study. David was taking coffee and biscuits. We accepted some and told him of our decision.

"Very wise," he nodded. "Robert, your former namesakes would have been proud of you. In a family like ours there have been many types of man. The schemers, the servants, the reprobates and many highly principled men – if you ask me, some of them too highly principled for their own damn good. Offered positions of service, they would resign over such principles rather than negotiate or seek to persuade. As a result they missed many excellent opportunities. I think you would have missed one too, had you declined." He paused to nibble a biscuit and mop crumbs from his lips with a napkin.

I took hold of Johnny's hand – I still couldn't bring myself to think of him as Robert – and squeezed it. He squeezed back.

"What've you got in mind for us then, as a way of 'serving our country'?" he asked.

David turned his grey eyes to look at us. "It's very simple really. I'm afraid that I can't explain the why, only the what. You've already discovered that inside the Centre for Genetic Rehabilitation is a solitary building for a patient who is kept isolated from the world. This is for their own good. Without divulging their identity, I can tell you that an attempt is to be made by certain individuals to release him. But they don't know what they're doing. It would be terribly dangerous. Now, if we were to interfere then they would know that we knew.

It would blow our informants' cover. What you have to do is to protect him and deny, should they ask, that it was we who asked you to do it. Is that clear?"

Johnny and I looked at each other. "Who are these people? The HRA?"

"No. Nobody you know."

"Are they dangerous? How will we defend ourselves?" I asked.

"Yeah, and who is this guy we're supposed to protect?" demanded Johnny.

"You'll have a chance to find that out when you get there. If you agree, we'll give you everything you need. I imagine you wish to discuss this between yourselves again. I've said enough for now. I must go – I have business in Whitehall. We can be in touch by phone."

David stood, smoothed his suit and held his hand out. There was an awkward moment while we realised what he wanted us to do, and shook hands with him. Then he left and we were alone.

Johnny displayed: "I'd really like to know who the mysterious inmate is. What do you say?"

"It's a test of our loyalty. He wants to be sure we're on his side," I typed into his arm. "But it could be really dangerous. What if we're caught and they blame us?"

"I get the feeling my dad wants us to negotiate."

"I'm sure it's a trap, Johnny. A set-up."

"I'm not so sure. I'm his son. His heir. You can see how he feels about stuff like that. Would he really put me in danger?"

"I don't know…" I typed.

"Tell you what, how about we ask for immunity from prosecution if anything goes wrong? And weapons? And full details of the expected raid? Don't you want to find out who's in that building?"

I gave up. I could see he was convinced this was a great adventure. And I wasn't about to let him go on his own.

That night we curled up together in my bed. It was the best night of my life. We didn't do anything but, clothed, hold each other all night and cry and laugh. Eventually, snaked in the double S shape together, with me at his back, we managed to get some sleep. We woke up completely in love with each other. And secure in the knowledge that our demands had been accepted by David Cecil.

Our instructions were left inside envelopes by the front door. They didn't say much. Just a time, and that we didn't need any weapons – just the skills we already had; or rather, Johnny had. The guards would take care of the rest.

At ten o'clock a car came to take us around a subdued M25 and off east to the CGR. The driver's radio droned on the whole way. A news announcer said there were now 8000 people inside the Zone – it was originally built for 5000. She said that many had already been taken from the CGR. The Zone had been sealed off from the rest of London. Nobody was allowed in or out. Another Zone would be set up in another part of the country to house further hybrids.

A minister assured listeners that those inside were being given proper medical attention and care. I wondered how likely this was. I thought about Mark Jarrett. He would know. I could phone him! I banged on the glass that separated us from the driver and asked him to stop at a payphone.

"Sorry, love," he said. "Instructions. No stopping. Can't be late."

After a while, the car stopped alongside a Gene Police van. We were told to get out and into the van – this felt really scary, as if we'd been duped and were now being led like cattle to the slaughter. But this was what our instructions said would happen. We'd be taken into the CGR in this way to avoid suspicion. The van continued on its journey and we lapsed into silence. It no longer seemed possible to talk.

"Johnny, is there any Internet? Can you email someone, like Mark? Tell them where we are?"

He shook his head grimly.

Our escorts paid scant attention to us. Soon, with a shock, I recognised that we were just a few hundred metres away from the CGR. There was the remains of the protest camp – muddy patches, a small rubbish dump, an abandoned campfire. I wondered what had happened to it and the people we'd sat round the circle with. That also seemed a long time ago.

The van passed through the gates, which shut behind us with an ominous clang. This was it. If we were in a trap, there was no getting out of it now. I felt for Johnny's hand: he had gone stiff with tension and was shaking nervously. The back doors opened and we stepped out. Four orderlies were there to receive us and escort us to our rooms. This was one thing I had not bargained for: we were now separated. I was alone in one room and he in another.

Suddenly, left on my own, in a featureless room, inside the place I had always dreaded, I was very afraid.

24. The Man in the Caged Building

Through the window of my cell, a different one than before, in the centre of a quadrangle, I could see the isolated building holding the mysterious inmate whom we had come to protect. A short shower had passed and thin sunlight glinted off its cage in rainbow colours. It looked mysterious and small, as if it might be larger on the inside than the outside. Opposite, to my relief, I spied Kestrella through another window. I waved and she waved back.

Between us we could see around the building. The quad was deserted. Our instructions said the break-out attempt would happen later today. But they didn't reveal how many would be attempting it or what they would do. All they did say was that my software skills would be sufficient to foil them.

I tested the network. Fine: although the protocols had been changed since I was last here, the new ones I'd been given worked perfectly. I didn't have the total access I did before with the protocols from my mother, but I could see through all the cameras in the immediate vicinity. I tested the Internet access. I was behind a government secure gateway with a triple firewall and masked IP addresses. There was no way I could get through. I sent my mum a message. There was no reply. I supposed that meant I wasn't supposed to contact her. Contrary to mission instructions.

I tested my door. Unlocked. I indicated this to Kestrella. She looked considerably happier than before on my digital zoom of her face.

It was after six and dark outside. I opened the door and peered into the corridor. I consulted the plan of the CGR that had been given us, turned right and right again, down a deserted corridor. Unlike the last time I was here, a deathly calm had settled on the place. There was no distant clanging of cell doors, no wails or shouts of inmates, no footsteps clanking up corridors, no alarms buzzing, monitors beeping or wheels squeaking. None of the good-humoured banter of Ahmed and Joseph. It was eerie. I arrived at a door leading into the quad. I fumbled with the protocols for a couple of seconds and then I was in the outside air. It was cold and damp.

I sprinted over and looked into Kestrella's room, but it was empty. Was she on her way out too? I checked all the CCTV cameras in the vicinity and made sure that none of them were pointing at me – best to be safe. Through one of them I caught sight of Kestrella. She appeared lost, wandering along a corridor.

I ran all round the caged building but there was nobody to be seen. Where were the promised guards? I checked my watch. Five minutes to go until the expected attack. I examined the radio-baffling cage and concluded that it was strong enough to climb up. In thirty seconds I was on the flat roof, five metres up. Looking down, I saw Kestrella enter the quad in the far corner. She saw me and I signalled to her to approach the door below. I didn't really have any idea what I was doing, but anything was better than sitting around.

I looked around the rooftop – the cage extended across it, but there was a trapdoor in the middle. Suddenly I felt something going on – inside me. Programs were being activated, instructions sent. There was a click and the trapdoor unlocked. I felt more changes inside and dimly heard a collective click from the quad as the locks jammed on all the doors entering it. Now I realised what was happening. Someone was hacking into my own system and using it to control remotely the local area security system. They were making it look like it was me doing it. But who was this person?

The air was split by the wailing of alarms. Through it I heard Kestrella shouting below. I peered over the edge.

"Let me in! Let me in!" She was pulling at the door to the building. It was the only option, for I could see inside the buildings surrounding the quad security guards racing towards the doors. I unlocked the door. She disappeared inside and slammed the door behind her.

It was then that the enormity of the situation hit me. She was inside with the mysterious inmate and I was on the roof wondering what to do. She could be in terrible danger. Now I had no choice. I looked through the trapdoor: a light shining from somewhere illuminated a drop of four metres. Oh well, nothing for it – I edged myself over the lip, hung from it for one second and then let myself go. It was only upon hitting the floor that I thought that I should have closed the trapdoor! Too late now, there was no way back up. I turned in the direction of the light. It shone through a partly open door which I approached and pushed wide. What I saw on the other side completely stunned me.

Kestrella looked up at me. "I–I don't think he's very well," she said.

She was standing over a cot in the middle of a dimly lit room. It was surrounded by humming instruments, monitoring or feeding a body almost completely concealed by bedding. To one side, an elderly nurse in protective clothing, clearly not expecting visitors, was keeping vigil. She shrank from our presence. Even from here I could see who the patient was. I approached the bed, aware of blinking lights reflecting off my screen and the regular bleeping of machines. Within here, the noises from outside were muffled.

I examined the two eyes gazing up at me. They were the colour of the sky on the horizon at dawn – giving an impression of the infinite void beyond, while concealing it. They were unmistakable, even to me – who had never taken much interest in politics. They belonged to the Prime Minister, Lionel Smith. They were deeply sunken into the mottled autumn-leaf-coloured skin that was stretched over his skull, and were full of meaning and intent. His voice was cracked and came propelled by great effort as if from far away.

"You've come just in time," he croaked.

"What do you mean?"

Suddenly I felt the same thing as before, inside me. As if I were being invaded, possessed, occupied. I tried to resist, marshalling my forces, but then I relaxed as I realised – resistance was wrong. A stream of information was being fed into my memory. The source of the information was the Prime Minister himself. I relayed it on to my screen so Kestrella could see it and watched her reaction as I read it too. The nurse went back to adjusting the controls on one of the machines.

At a trigger from the Prime Minister a pre-recorded message played through my speakers. It was a much stronger version of the voice we'd just heard: "I don't know who you are, but the fact that you are here means that I have been successful. I hope you will forgive me for what I have done to you, by bringing you here and giving you this information. I have no idea whether it will be of any use to you and whether my ultimate aim will be successful. There isn't much time. The programs that you have used will keep the guards outside for a while but not for long.

"I have been kept here for four months in isolation, completely cut off from the outside world. Why? Because I am a hybrid. But how can I be a hybrid, you're asking yourselves? Aren't all hybrids young or recent? Evidently not. I first experienced the onset of the disease six years ago, a few years before most other victims. I discovered later that this is because there are always a few isolated cases at the beginning of an epidemic before it spreads to the general population. At this stage, a virus is unstable and trying to find a foothold in its new host – at that point RTGV was able to infect people of any age.

"At the time, I was deputy leader of my party, which was in opposition. Out of embarrassment and fear I kept my condition secret, trying to treat it myself. After a while it became more severe, but I found a sympathetic doctor whom I could trust to keep my condition confidential.

"What is the nature of my condition? Well, since I was a small child, parallel to my interest in politics, I was interested in computers, especially the Internet. I wrote software, collected computers and servers, and later had my own business managing Internet searches and security. It was inevitable that this was the direction in which my condition would develop.

"My Internet connection became part of me. My consciousness spread throughout the Internet. It seemed like an incredible blessing, a sign. I experienced vast knowledge, and used it ruthlessly to become firstly the leader of my party and then, by securing a landslide victory, Prime Minister of the country. The future was mine. And nobody knew how I had done it. Can you believe this?"

We were startled by a commotion outside. The guards had evidently broken through the doors on to the quad and were now trying to open the door to this building. How long would it hold? I stared across his body at Kestrella, at her expression of incredulity. But the pre-recorded lecture was continuing at its own pace.

"However, my success was not to last. The disease had become a pandemic. Nobody else in government seemed to be afflicted by it. They were all wanting to respond to the public demand for protection. I tried to preach understanding, tolerance, treatment. I was certain that one day a cure would be found. Although my own condition was getting worse and becoming more painful and hard to conceal, I was sure we could get enough funds to defeat it. But other countries were looking at us and demanding immediate action. Our trading partners were pulling away. Airlines were refusing to bring passengers here. The market for electronics products was collapsing. The economy was in a nosedive and with it my authority. Something had to be done, and in a Cabinet meeting I was overruled. And then they found out my secret.

"So they constructed the Centre for Genetic Rehabilitation. They created the Gene Police. And they brought me here and isolated me in this building, specially shielded from all types of radiation and connections so there was no way I could access the

Internet or the public, and stop what they were doing, for I know secrets they don't want to get out. I still had a sizeable group of supporters. Ever since then, disconnected from much of the rest of myself, I have fought my slow decline. But all I have done is to stave off the inevitable."

There were shouts outside and a banging on the door.

"Before Hunter Cracke and his minions put me in here, I could see what was going to happen and developed a plan. I wrote some software using fuzzy logic. I gave the program an aim: to bring somebody here to rescue me, somebody who had the capacity to accept what I needed to tell them. I gave it as many tools as possible to do this, but no definite scheme or plan to get the person here. It had to work that out for itself by trial and error and replication – like the virus itself. I don't know how it brought you here, by what system of smoke and mirrors, concealment and incentives. It would have had to have infiltrated networks, created false documents, manipulated databases, who knows what. To me that's not important, though it must be to you. What is important is that you're here. Look at me—"

Kestrella and I could see the urgency in his face. He coughed and his whole body was racked in pain. For a second I thought it was his last breath, but no. He was trying to speak. We leant close to listen, and Kestrella took the opportunity to hold my hand. His voice was as thin as the rustle of wind in dry grass.

"I know that they plan to exterminate all the hybrids. The plan was hatched months ago." He coughed again. "I know the hybrids aren't a real danger. The real danger's fear – and economic collapse. Now you're here, there's a route to the Internet. Via the trapdoor you left open. Take it – feel who I am."

Suddenly something was triggered. And I felt my inner eye opening up to a new vista. Naturally, I had been within the Internet before, planting my files all over the place. But this was different; it wasn't as if I was journeying along the connections that make up the Internet. I was the cables, the signals, the protocols, software, servers, relays. The exchanges, processors, satellite dishes, boosting stations, aerials, modems. You name it, it's as if I was stretching out to cover the planet. Not just its surface, but communication satellites in orbit around the earth. Before this happened I was a tiny little insect the size of a louse. Afterwards I was bigger than a whale. Before this I was a piece of lichen growing on the side of a tree. Afterwards I felt like the entire tree. Before this I was a child playing in the dirt in sub-Saharan Africa. Afterwards I seemed to be Africa itself.

At least, this was what it felt like. I could look down metaphorically and see myself inside this tiny room in a tiny group of buildings, in a tiny muddy corner of a small country on this medium-sized planet. I saw how vulnerable and small and pathetic I looked. I saw Kestrella standing next to me, another insignificant and powerless individual, ignorant of virtually everything going on in the world. Through various CCTV cameras I saw the guards struggling outside. And I began to get a sense of everything that was contained on all of these servers, hard drives, tapes and optical drives. All of this overwhelming information, far too much for any of these human beings to appreciate even one per cent of one per cent of. But now, with all the processors at my command, I realised it was theoretically possible for me to do this. I forced my consciousness back into the room as I became aware of a local threat. The guards had broken through the outside door.

Kestrella was staring at me with an expression I'd never seen before. As if she was looking at a complete stranger. Suddenly the Prime Minister emitted an awful noise that seemed to come from below the floor, spasming up and down as he expelled his last breath and came to rest. With this breath, he had given me my new life. His memories and his abilities were now mine to access. But what was I to do with them?

Without thinking, I shut off all the electricity. The lights cut and all the background noises ceased. The nurse's scream sliced the pitch darkness. I still had Kestrella's hand although she was trying to pull it away from my grip.

"It's all right, Kestrella," I whispered. "Don't worry."

I led her to where I knew the door into the room was and crouched down beside it. Immediately, four guards entered, armed and carrying powerful torches. Four more came in via the trapdoor. I made a whimpering noise and nudged Kestrella, who copied me. They escorted us out and across the courtyard. I adopted the body language of a defeated person.

"I'm sorry, I'm sorry!" I kept saying. "I failed. I'm so sorry. I don't know what happened…"

They took us to an office and left us there. Kestrella and I said nothing to each other. After a short while, my mother entered, crisp as a sentry.

"He's dead," she said curtly. "I suppose that solves the problem one way or another."

I stared at her glumly.

"Are you OK, Johnny?" she asked.

"I – I think so," I said.

Now, all puffed up, my father came in – followed, astonishingly, by Jacquelyn, almost in tears. I noticed immediately that he and my mother greeted each other with exaggerated formality.

"Smith's dead," repeated my mum.

"Ah," said my father. "That's a shame. A big shame."

"I don't know," she said. "It's one less thing to worry about. We can close the place down now."

"There's a silver lining to everything, I suppose," he replied, drily. Then he looked at me. "Feeling OK, Robert?"

I nodded, my attention elsewhere. Meanwhile, Jacquelyn and Kestrella had rushed towards each other and embraced.

"Oh, my darling! Oh, my darling!" Jacquelyn was crying.

"Maman! But how did you get here?" asked Kestrella.

"Oh, Kestrella. I'm so sorry! I made a mistake!"

"Calm down, Maman. What do you mean?"

Jacquelyn took a few gulps of air, then began. "After you left, I realised I made the wrong decision. You're more important to me than Thom," she said. "Really you are. I was stupid. I was – I don't know – under some kind of spell. I realised I should have come with you, not let you go on your own."

"Yes. That's true. But how did you find me?"

"I looked at Johnny's emails. I traced you to David's place and he brought me here."

"Maman. Please tell me you weren't in love with that moron after all?" Kestrella asked.

Her mother frowned. "What is love, Kestrella? Sometimes emotions get the better of you. That's all I can say for now. Do you forgive me, sweetheart?"

They hugged again. "I'm glad you came," said Kestrella.

My father spoke to us. "Time to leave," he said. "You've both done very well."

"We have?" I asked him. "Are you aware what's happened?"

"Don't worry," he said. "It's not your fault we didn't catch anyone. Perhaps the kidnappers got wind of your presence and that's why they never showed. Or perhaps our intelligence was faulty. His death is not your fault either. We knew he didn't have much time left."

As I followed them out I understood that he didn't understand – in fact, nobody knew about Lionel Smith's plan and how well it had worked. Nobody but Kestrella and I. I was wearing the mantle of the Prime Minister. A Prime Minister who had been imprisoned and effectively killed by members of his own party. Was I being melodramatic to call this the first case of political assassination since the English Civil War?

Lionel Smith had given me all his memories and his powers. I let the knowledge sink into me as I silently slipped into a waiting Mercedes with Kestrella, Jacquelyn and my dad.

But my mum had called my father back. She was speaking urgently to him at the door. I turned up the volume of my microphone in an attempt to hear them. But all I could catch were phrases such as: "You can't take him!" and "But he can't stay here." It was as if my mother were objecting – strongly – to the fact that my father was taking me away.

It was a fait accompli however. He climbed into the vehicle and she was waving a reluctant farewell – at me – as it began to speed away from the CGR into the drizzling darkness. I did not wave back.

I was instead absorbed with Hunter Cracke's plan – to exterminate all the hybrids in the Zone. Perhaps only I could stop it.

25. Reunited

I snuggled up to Maman. It felt so good to be with her again. I could hardly believe we were out of that horrible place.

"Maman?" I asked.

"Mmm, *ma chérie*?"

"Are we going home now?"

"I wish we could. But you would be sent to the Zone if so."

"But we're not going back to the HRA, are we?" I said. "I have a feeling they're going to be busted."

"Really? But – no, in any case. I think we need to spend time together, just you and I."

That was so good to hear.

David said, from the front passenger seat, "Remember, you are now officially dead, Kestrella, and your mother is listed as missing. You can't go home to your father, but I'm happy to let both of you stay at my house for the time being. And Robert too, of course."

That was wonderful news. I looked up at Maman and she smiled at me.

"But, David, don't you mind harbouring hybrids?"

"Not in your case. Things are not always black and white, Kestrella. There are factions within the government. I don't have to believe all of the government's propaganda."

"Are you part of a faction that sympathises with hybrids?" I asked him cautiously.

"Let's say more so than Cracke," he said.

"But you're the one responsible for drawing up all the anti-hybrid legislation! You told me so!" I cried.

"That doesn't mean I necessarily approve of it," he replied, with an odd sort of smile. "I was following Cracke's instructions."

I didn't understand. It was politics. I felt so confused. The last few weeks had been like a whirlwind. All I really knew for sure was that I had my mother back. I gave up asking questions and let my head fall against her fake fur coat.

I looked at Johnny, the so-special boy I had come to love. He was staring out of the window into the speeding darkness. He seemed to be lost in his own world. I wondered what was going on inside him. His screen was blank, his posture firm and formal, his bearing haughty and aloof.

"Johnny, are you all right?" I asked.

"I'm fine, thank you," he replied, too fast and without turning, in his same cold, impersonal voice. "And as I keep telling you, my name is not Johnny."

What did he mean? Something had happened in that small room, beyond what I'd perceived. Whatever it was I had no idea, but it seemed to have changed his personality. I reached out to touch him, but there was no response.

Tears began to fall from my eyes. He didn't seem to notice and my sobbing increased. Maman stroked my head as the car sped back to Twickenham. She probably thought it was because I was relieved that we were back together.

"Johnny," I tried again. "Johnny, tell me what's wrong…"

Finally, Johnny spoke. "My name is Lionel."